BUILD

UNIVERSES

Richard D. Bateson

Jonny Jenson and the Last Pharaoh

Copyright ©2021 Richard D. Bateson

© 2021 **Europe Books** | London
www.europebooks.co.uk – info@europebooks.co.uk

ISBN 979-12-201-1035-8
First edition: June 2021

Distribution for the United Kingdom: **Vine House Distribution ltd**

Printed for Italy by Rotomail Italia
Finito di stampare nel mese di giugno 2021
presso Rotomail Italia S.p.A. - Vignate (MI)

Jonny Jenson and the Last Pharaoh

Chapter One

The museum's great court was rather impressive for a small irrelevant nation on a technologically backward, carbon-fuelled planet. It was the end of rather a long day and fortunately there was no queue for the exhibition. Rather amusingly the exhibition was entitled 'Book of the Dead'. The man smiled, little did they know that not all the Pharaohs were dead and some had pursued interesting career changes.

He had time to kill so he watched the introductory movie for kids. Mad, superstitious lot the Egyptians he thought. So many irrelevant gods. He liked the Great Devourer the best though – he looked a bit like a crocodile, lion and hippo all thrown together. At least the ancient Egyptians had a good imagination or sense of humour, he couldn't decide which.

He was the last person. They were closing up behind him. The English were too polite to hurry him along. In the third room he found what he was looking for. It was just as he had been told. A large scroll about a yard long written on ancient papyrus. Minuscule hieroglyphics scrawled all over it by some very patient but long deceased scribe. At one end a Pharaoh sat on a throne holding a shining sceptre. Behind him and a small jackal-headed black statue stretched a line of obscure gods; baboon-headed, hawk-headed, crocodile-headed and other unfathomable headed things. In front of the throne lay a prostate crowd of worshippers. This was definitely it. The product of a deranged mind he thought.

He quickly placed a pair of filter plugs up his nose and activated the knockout gas canister control in his pocket. That would take care of the guards. A quick pulse from the electromagnetic disruptor neutralised the alarm system and the sonic knife cut effortlessly through the plate glass. Two minutes later he stumbled out of the pillared front door of the

British Museum a cardboard tube under his arm and his foot in plaster. The leaden grey clouds were optimistically starting to clear. A trip to the beach was definitely in order.

Chapter Two

Two days later

It was a hot sunny day and the beach was full of tourists. The small fishing boats bobbed up and down carelessly in St. Ives harbour as Jonny rushed back to his parent's cafe. He was late back from his surf break and he was still dripping wet. Hopefully his dad would not mind him being a bit late. The surf was great today and last night's storms out at sea had created some great rollers. Anyway, it was nearly the end of the school holidays so who cared? Jonny chucked his surfboard down by the entrance to the blue and white cafe and rushed inside. The cafe was packed with families munching fish and chips, scampi and burgers and the steaks which sizzled on the terrace barbeque. Seagulls whirled around the terrace eyeing people's scampi. His dad glared at him as he rushed by plates in hand

'You're late again! Good surf? Could you help that gentleman out by the bar?'

'Yea was great. Sure, no problem,' Jonny replied turning to look at the bar.

A tall, muscular man in a strange T-shirt which read 'Save the Ice Leopards...' sat on the barstool. His foot was in plaster and he held a long cardboard tube. Probably a poster from the nearby Tate art museum Jonny thought.

'Hey kid. Could you do me a favour and look after this for me. Only for an hour or two? Don't want to mess it up on the beach. Sand gets everywhere. And I'll take a Coke too please,' he grinned.

An Ozzie or Kiwi accent maybe? Maybe not. Still, he was not from round here.

'I'll put your poster in the office. Nice day for sunbathing.'

'Yes, great beach you have here. One of my favourites.'

'Surf's better on the other beach though.' Then again, the guy didn't look like a surfer, more like a tanned lounge lizard.

'Your dad own the cafe? Not diet ... I'll take original. Don't often get real sugar.'

Jonny served him an original Coke and looked at his bandaged foot.

'Yes. He has had it ages. Busy in summer but dead in winter. How did you do the foot?'

'Tobogganing ... but it's a long cold story. See you later kid.'

Tobogganing in summer? Not too feasible thought Jonny. Probably, like most tourists, just got drunk and fell over or something. As the man left he read the back of his T-shirt '... from eating you! ... visit Necras IV!' Snow Leopards Jonny had seen on the BBC. Elusive and difficult to photograph. But what were Ice Leopards? He would ask the man later.

The fake tobogganer hopped out to a lounger on the beach and sat in the full hot sun. No oil or sun-cream thought Jonny, complete head-case. As his dad would say, 'Probably some stupid know-all, banker or lawyer down from London. Let the idiot burn under the Cornish sun.'

Chapter Three

One week earlier

'Hi this is Antonoff Werhofer XVII welcoming you to the first round of the Spiral Rim Extreme Sports X Cup sponsored by Intergalactic Mega-Hillton Hotels. We bring you the competition live from the icy slopes of Devil's Peak on Necras IV. What's today shaping up like Dec?'

'Yes Ant. Today promises an action packed qualifier – the first of five rounds to be declared the Extreme Sports X Cup champion and winning five billion Andurian crypto-dollars prize money ... plus a lifetime of free holidays on Megastar Galactic cruises. What's the course like Ant?'

'Well, it's a bit chilly out there Dec. Touch above 80 Kelvin, the sun is coming up in a minute and surface sublimation starts. The nitrogen slopes are gonna be very, very fast. Sixty courageous competitors must descend the ten mile almost vertical Devil's Peak and avoid the fatal seracs and crevasses. The ten fastest finishers on Devil's Plain qualify.'

'Hey Ant. I've a major star here to talk us through it. Walmoose Whaloo triple champion before his retirement.'

Those dual clone presenters were always pretty smarmy and nauseous thought Rex. Still, they brought in the viewers and helped make it a big ticket event across the whole galactic sector. They reckoned over one trillion viewers tuned into the final. Bigger than the Galactic Super-Bowl or the bloody circuses of Maximus V. Viewers loved accidents and in the Extreme X Cup death was a bit more subtle, artistic and spectacular than the poor gladiators getting eaten in those circuses. Walmoose Whaloo appeared on the view screen. He looked in visibly bad shape despite all that retirement and endless cruises. Half his body had been rebuilt after that failed canyon jump a few years ago. It looked like his surgeon had drunk too many Sirius Mega cocktails before the operation.

'Yah. Zee first event sorts out the men from the boys. Any fear on zee ice descent and you lose balance and control. Zat is fatal.'

'Yes, Walmoose that's great. I will remind viewers they have a 51% accident rate and a 9% mortality rate on the luge event. Galactic Index is still open for sports betting for ten more minutes to take viewers bets. It's tax free folks!'

'Yes, Ant and they are also taking bets on the number of people eaten by Ice Leopards. Remember Dan Ousleeger last year? Broke a leg and got eaten ... what a good sport!'

'Dec, our viewers will know that Ice Leopards are now an IGWF protected species. Their breeding numbers are falling and if you want to make a charitable donation to their survival the Inter Galactic Wildlife Federation number is at the bottom of the screen.'

Why was Rex doing this insane event? Still it was too late to pull out now. If he did not compete then friendly Rama would kill him anyway, and probably torture him first, for all the money he owed him. Rama, so he had heard, was a torture aficionado. Somebody once told him 'don't mess with ancient Egyptians when it comes to torture ... they really know where to put a red-hot poker'. This was the quickest way to clear his debts and he did not even need to win ... just finish stage III. Rama was generally a man of his word.

He sat on a bench inside the transparent force dome with the other competitors and waited his turn to be called by the race Marshals. Fear hung in the air but nobody wanted to show it. A mix of professional sportsmen, adventurers and chancers from all over the Galactic Rim. Perhaps thirty or forty different races were represented from humans, Mega-Trolls, Octi-men to Blue-Goo. What sort of pressure suit did Blue-Goo wear

Rex thought with no arms or legs? How did he control his luge for that matter? Unsurprisingly the toilet was fully occupied. After the first descent was shown a queue quickly formed outside.

'See you at the bottom in pieces big boy!' taunted Elmer Diablilo as he marched past Rex in his black pressure suit, luge under his arm. He was second in the draw and Rex third. Some novice rich kid Vegan called Schumachen was first. He was apparently doing it for thrills. An adrenaline junky Rex thought. Apparently, it was best to be among the first in the draw. There was less chance of being attacked by Ice Leopards. Huge icy beasts with triple sets of fangs they generally they took a while to congregate on the course. He could not imagine what there was to eat out there but someone had told him that the second dominant indigenous species on the planet was a really cute icy bunny, that was fated to not run as fast as Ice Leopards. Being among the first in the draw was faster but route finding was more difficult. Elmer Diablilo was a pro and one of the favourites. He was a finalist last year and nearly won. If he could get close to his time – without hitting a rock or being eaten – he would get through.

Rex watched Schumachen on the holo-screen as the floating camera droids followed his yellow pressure suit lying on the small luge down the run. He looked insignificant on the scale of Devils Peak, a cone shaped grey icy mountain under a near jet black sky. The run itself started near the summit with a near two mile almost vertical chute section about the width of a small aircar – the Devil's Crotch it was called. After that near frictionless descent, gliding over sublimating nitrogen and methane, competitors attained almost 300 miles an hour. The mountain then gradually levelled out after a further eight to ten miles into an icy rubble strewn plain towards the finish. Crevasses in the icy plateau spewed out clouds of icy nitrogen and methane crystals to add to the spectacle for those billions of viewers.

Schumachen started well but halfway down the chute obviously panicked. His luge started to tremble and then as he struggled to regain control he flipped over and ricocheted like a pinball down the Devils Crotch before crashing into some spires of jagged ice near the exit. The competitors in the room went suddenly silent. Medic droids flew in to retrieve the body, their flashing lights illuminating the mountain. The presenters swung into action as the body count on the screen went from zero to one.

'Well Ant, that sure… sure is a shame for Stefan Schumachen. His folks back home on Vega III will sure be disappointed. I think he panicked a bit there don't you. A good luger just keeps calm.'

'Yes Dec. It's a shame for him. His coach said he had good potential. Anyways a lot to get through today. Next up is another boy from the Vegan system … Elmer Diablilo this year's Vegan Extreme Cross champion and last year's finalist! Good luck Elmer!'

'Too bad Schumachen. What a total looser!' mocked Elmer Diablilo before he strode out of the dome to the start. Total confidence or complete idiot, thought Rex. He took a few more Relax-Aid tablets to calm himself down but the dispenser told him he had already maxed out the prescription. Elmer Diablilo had a clear run and made it look easy. He navigated his way through all the icy obstacles and clocked up 259 miles per hour average speed. The mood in the competitors dome lightened somewhat.

The Marshal tapped Rex on the shoulder. It was his turn. He picked up his luge and turned on his red pressure suit. It seemed too flimsy to offer much protection from a high-speed collision. He stepped through the force wall and onto the mountain and walked the ten paces, across the slippery, icy surface to the start of the chute. A couple of yellow vested Marshals helped him into position, asked him if he was okay and the starting droid held him ready for the push-off.

'Ready,' muttered Rex. He wasn't though. Never would be. He would have much rather been sipping a Sirius Mega cocktail in the hotel whirl-bath with that cute Andurian news reporter he had met. He could not decide whether to focus on the event or let the Relax-Aid tablets take effect.

'3, 2, 1 ... go!' the starting droid released him into the dark icy chute. He held steady and tried not to panic as the speed increased ... 50, 100, 135 ... His helmet display gave him all the gory technical detail as he raced across the ice almost falling vertically towards the endless plain far below. The luge shook as he absorbed the pits and bumps of the icy terrain. The light atmosphere offered little wind resistance. He controlled the vibration and focused on following Elmer Diablilo's rapidly sublimating tracks. He swerved around a couple of small seracs and jumped a micro crevasse at the exit of the chute. Rex breathed a sigh of relief and headed towards the bright lights of the finish. He had made it! Two seconds later he caught the rail of his luge on the edge of a small block of ice and spun out of control. 'Shit! Knew I should have stayed in that whirl-bath,' he thought to himself as everything went black.

Chapter Four

The week before that

The small city of Vigilstrammer on Juno sat like a pearl on the shores of a beautiful luminescent blue lake. Rex liked the feel of university towns – their historic buildings, the uncommercial air unspoiled by the rest of the intergalactic rat race, the occasional badly dressed boffin walking down the street and of course the pretty students on bikes. He missed it, even though he had dropped out of his Stanfield University course years ago much to the dismay of his mother. Engineering had proved not to be his thing he had decided. He preferred to use things, preferably without paying, rather than building them and figuring out how they worked.

Rex had told Rama that time machines don't exist. Rama had other ideas and said that in fact he knew exactly how to get one. All Rex had to do was use his lovely wit and charms to get his hands on it. Rama knew Rex's reputation for showing people a good time and his intimate knowledge of where to find a good Sirus Mega cocktail in the dingiest backwaters of the Galaxy.

It was easy to be Professor Mitchell's new best friend. He didn't get out much and was so absent minded that he couldn't remember any of his old students anyway. A visit to his favourite restaurant followed by the Vigilstrammer Erotic Girly Bar (unfortunately the only one in town Rex noted) and five or six bottles of Ligronian wine later and he was Rex's best buddy.

'Rex I really appreciate one of my best students coming to visit me,' he slurred. 'And you've done well for yourself. I am proud. I love this Ligronian wine. I can never afford it myself.'

The Professor looked even scruffier now after a few drinks. His grey hair and beard were tousled and some of his scruffy shirt buttons had popped open round his large belly. Since the Professor spent most his life in his lab, he clearly preferred to spend money improving his experiments than in the fancy designer shops on the Vigilstrammer waterfront. A new sub-neutrino spectrometer was evidently far more interesting than a pretentious Erno Zegelmeyer shirt.

'Still working on time-travel Professor?' Rex decided it was time to get to the point. He had looked the Professor up and he saw he had not published much recently except a few obscure theory papers that nobody cited. Rex couldn't even understand the abstracts of these papers but the titles sounded funky like 'Indeterministic Causal Violation in an N-fold Space-Time String Continuum' and 'Quantum Mechanical Equilibria in Generalised Causal Space-Time Conservation'. All tediously academic and confusing. Rex was only interested in the practical applications.

'You mean causal violation? Yes of course ... but hush, hush because they don't like it.' He answered trying to put a finger to his lips and swaying a bit and almost sticking it up his nose.

'Who are they? The university? The government?' asked Rex.

'No, no,' the Professor looked anxiously around him. 'The Chrono Police!' Rex had no idea what he was talking about but the Professor was now apparently eager to show him something now his favourite topic was being discussed. He became very agitated and staggered to his feet and picked up his coat to leave.

The Professor was semi-paralytic and Rex felt he had perhaps overdone it by slipping the Ruskovan vodka shots into the last few glasses of wine. They staggered a few hundred yards away from the university towards the lake and approached an old, decrepit chocolate shop. Rows of fancy, expensive looking chocolates were lined up in the window. Vigilstrammer was well known among interstellar tourists for its specialty chocolates. It was too late to be open, so the Professor fumbled around for his keys.

'They will never find it here,' said the Professor drunkenly swaying, 'and it would take them hours to get past all this chocolate anyway'. Rex was a bit confused but helped the Professor find the right key.

They passed through the dark shop and through a door and down some creaking wooden stairs. At the bottom was a robust looking steel door with a retina pass. Rex held the Professor steady for the scan. Once inside he flicked on the lights.

Inside was not what Rex expected or maybe having known the Professor for two hours he should have expected. No white shining lab but just a damp old basement full of crazy looking machinery and tables cluttered with electronics. A white board stood in the corner with some mad physics diagrams. He vaguely recognised some complex numbers, Argand diagrams, matrices and differential equations. It looked like quantum mechanics, relativity and other stuff he did not and never would understand. It was all a bit gloomy and underwhelming. At least the Professor could have improved the lighting or painted the dilapidated plaster walls white.

'This is it – the Causal Flux Generator,' announced the Professor with a drunken sweep of his arm, almost falling in the process. Rex stared at a small glass box with huge power cables connected to it. Inside a small blue light flickered amidst a spidery network of filaments.

'A time machine?' asked Rex a bit underwhelmed. He had been expecting some shiny new spaceship or rather time-ship or something. At least he had been hoping for something that looked the part.

'Not a time machine! Conventional hyperdrives are time machines. Faster than light travel allows time travel – any idiot can do that. Relativistic exchange of space for time and what not. How do you think space travel works these days?'

'Yea well of course,' Rex nodded enthusiastically. He always tried to feel genuinely enthusiastic in the presence of new technology. It was always meant to make your life easier right?

'No,' the Professor paused excitedly, 'this allows causality violation. Violation of cause and effect. Generates a randomised quantum field so you can actually go back and change things!'

Rex looked at him blankly. He had always assumed that's what time travel meant. He propped the Professor onto a stool before he completely collapsed.

'That's what the Chrono Police don't like. Think it's dangerous changing things. Quite right too probably. Chronological violation can set past, present and future down a different path.' He muttered more softly now '...but they do like chocolate though!' He smiled and collapsed on the bench. Rex looked at the Causal Flux Generator and wondered what to do with it. Hopefully it had an instruction manual.

Chapter Five

A large shadow loomed over Rex blocking the sun. More precisely two shadows.

'Do you mind?' he said in slight annoyance. He hated his crucial sunbathing minutes being spoiled.

'Captain Rex Rogers we have reason to believe you are in possession of an unlicensed Chronological Violation Device.'

'A what?' Rex jumped with surprise. So surprised in fact the remains of his Coke and ice cubes spilt over his trunks causing him to wince. It was very refreshing but in the wrong sort of way.

'A Causal Flux Generator, Sir.'

Rex tried squinting at them to get a better look but the sun made it painful. He obviously had a big problem. These must be the Chrono Police he thought. But how did they find him in small seaside town on the toe of an insignificant country on a virtually unknown, technologically backward planet that would not be listed in any of the major galactic tourist guides for another one thousand years.

'No idea what you are talking about. You must have the wrong guy. Mistaken identity or something.' He got his brain functioning again from beach holiday mode. 'Just down here on holiday from London with the kids. Look there they are...' He pointed to some small children playing in the sea nearby. The shadows hesitated and slowly turned their heads to look at the children.

'Listen, Sir. We don't make mistakes,' they continued, turning back round. But Rex was gone. Running or rather hopping as fast as he could towards the cafe. Rex looked back. They were massive – a clear head taller than humans. They wore dark overcoats and had dark glasses and a funny translucent sheen to their perfectly white skin. Suspiciously like something off that Matrix movie, Rex had watched on his last trip to Earth a few years ago. He guessed the bulky items under their coats were probably not mobile phones. He ran as fast as he could and tried to think of a plan.

Chapter Six

Rex burst in through the cafe door. The lunchtime crowds had gone and Jonny was sweeping up. He leapt at the boxes of confectionary behind the counter.

'Kit-Kat – too much biscuit. Mars – too much caramel stuff.'

'What you up to?' Jonny demanded. 'Hey. You're not allowed back there.'

'Milka bars ... perfect!' Rex grabbed a fist full and started tearing off the wrappers. Jonny looked on in amazement. 'Help me out here kiddo. Open them all up. I'll buy the box.'

Rex glanced at Jonny's surfboard by the door. 'Can I borrow that too? Need to paddle over to my ship. I'll bring it back later.'

Two large shadows appeared at the frosted glass door. 'That's them,' Rex announced. Rex cracked open the door slightly and quickly thrust a couple of dozen Milka bars at them. He slammed the door and threw a chair behind it. There were squeals and snorts of delight as the chocolate was wolfed down by the overcoats.

Jonny was astonished. The giant men outside sounded like nothing he had heard before. Like enormous pigs. They obviously appreciated Swiss chocolate.

Rex ran to the backdoor with the surfboard under his arm, dodging round a portly, red sunbather exiting the gents. He hopped as fast as he could towards the shore, past the sandcastles, children and umbrellas.

Chapter Seven

'Hey, you forgot your poster!' Jonny waved the tube above his head as he sprinted down the beach. He saw that Rex was struggling to get on the surfboard with his bandaged foot. A pathetic landlubber he thought to himself and decided to take pity on him.
'Get on the board,' he said. 'I'll push you. You hold the poster. Which boat is it?' Rex pointed trying not to fall off the other side of the surfboard for the fourth time. 'That's your boat?' exclaimed Jonny laughing. 'How you gonna escape those guys on that?'

It looked like a cross between an old Chinese junk and something straight out of Pirates of the Caribbean. The boat appeared to be built of old dark wood and the prow had a smiling figurine of a busty mermaid. The sails somehow fluttered even though there was no wind and it was not moving. Rex felt rather pleased with himself. He had used all his (rather limited) artistic tendencies, with Dennis's help, to come up with his best holo-camouflage ever. Really, he kind of wished his space-freighter looked like that all the time but it was probably impractical for spaceflight.

'Actually, it goes very fast. It has Vegan G5 fusion afterburners – they are used in galactic drag racers.'

Jonny looked at him like he was insane. Still, you had to be rather strange to sail an unseaworthy wooden junk around in the cold English waters.

They got to within a couple of metres of the ship and then somehow kept going and passed through the wooden hull. On the other side was the scared and pitted metallic hull of the Centennial Eagle. It floated mostly submerged in the water like a submarine with a hatch lying open at the top. Sure, it needed a new paint job but it was all temporary until Rex could afford the gleaming Suncruiser star-yacht he had seen at the boat show last year.

Jonny was amazed. 'Wow what a disguise! Like something on Dr. Who. It's a spaceship, right? Your ship looks like a bit of a rusty old dump though. Is it safe?' Jonny, being a kid, seemed to take seeing a spaceship in his stride. In fact, having being subjected to a diet of his elder brother's science fiction movies since birth he had recently been extremely disappointed at school to learn that mankind had only made it as far as the moon and not to Tatooine as he previously thought.

The analogy with Dr. Who was a good one thought Rex but Dr. Who's time machine on TV seemed a bit more reliable. This was one of Rex's typical understatements. Since the last time-jump, or causal displacement as Dennis liked to call it, a few days ago his ears had only just recovered. The ship seemed to dangerously vibrate and ring like a bell when using the Flux Generator. Rex thought the ship was going to fall apart and irritatingly lots of his precious Vegan china had been smashed on board. Clearly there was something not quite right with the Professor's technology.

Chapter Eight

They clambered through the hatch. Jonny was eager to see the inside of a real spaceship. Rex helped him drag in the wet surfboard.

'This arrived marked for you' stated Dennis blandly. It was a recorded delivery sub-ethergram with a rather grandiose stamp on it.

Rex took a quick look at it and exhaled slowly. How had they caught up with him here? It was his unpaid minibar bill from the Mega Hillton on Nexus IV. He had escaped paying it and avoided an awkward checkout conversation by virtue of having his foot ripped off. Apparently, his credit card had been declined. It made impressive reading ... fifteen bottles of Vothschild IV millennium champagne, ten bottles of vintage Ligronian wine, the best Belgossian caviar, specialty canapés ... total 190 thousand Andurian dollars or thereabouts. Politely it indicated that they would accept payment in a range of galactic currencies. Complete rip-off thought Rex. How could a night of hard partying with those pretty Andurian news girls cost so much money? Rama would have to cover him and add it to his colossal debts.

'Cool robot. What's his name? Looks really retro!' said Jonny.

'Dennis. Yea cool styling. I designed that as well. Forbidden Planet. You seen that movie? It's a classic,' Rex replied screwing up the minibar bill and chucking it out the hatch.

Jonny had never seen Forbidden Planet. Star Wars and the Alien movies were as far back as his sci-fi knowledge went. The grey metallic robot was taller even than Rex and had a huge glass dome as a head with two funny looking rotating antennae attached. Under the dome strange coloured lights flickered as if Dennis was thinking hard about something.

Dennis hated his current look. Rex had watched a very old, cheesy Earth film called Forbidden Planet and decided it would be a laugh if Dennis looked like Robbie the Robot for a while. Dennis or Droid Engineered with Nuclear Nanotechnology Induction System (DENNIS) was composed of billions of self-organising nano components and could change his shape at will and look like whatever he wanted. He was the latest model in distributed physical cybernetics from the Syrus Droid Foundries and could reconfigure himself to be anything from CP3O (another of Rex's favourites) to a Vegan teapot (although rather a large one). Rex had won him in a game of poker with Lazard Bond, self-proclaimed mega buyout king, a few months ago. All these retro film robot roles really pissed him off but he guessed that was what he was designed for.

'Nice to meet you young Sir,' greeted Dennis. 'Would you like a cold beverage after your swim?' A large mouth below the dome flashed in a rainbow of colours in synchrony as he spoke. He handed Jonny a towel.

'Later Dennis. There are bad guys out there. Fire up the engines and get this crate airborne pronto,' ordered Rex.

'Where to Sir Rex?'

'Omega.'

'Which Omega Sir? There are at least ten of them. Very popular name for a planet or star system for that matter.'

'The one with all the horrible water.'

'That would be Omega V, VI or IX. They are all waterworlds Sir.'

'Dunno,' replied Rex exasperated. This was the problem with robots he thought. They knew all the options and possibilities but often found it difficult to extrapolate what he was talking about and what might constitute useful information. It was probably just his problem that he had circular conversations with robots since nobody else seemed to complain too much. Maybe robots just lacked curiosity.

'I guess that you want Omega V Sir for the competition? But you know your foot is not yet healed Sir and exercise is inadvisable.'

Dennis clanked off down the corridor towards the flight deck. He found it difficult to circulate as Robbie the Robot around the confines of the spaceship. He had tried rescaling the design but essentially clunky metal legs and a big domed glass head with irrelevant antenna were a stupid idea.

Chapter Nine

Jonny followed Rex in the opposite direction towards the engine room. Based on all the movies he had seen he could categorise spaceships into several types based on their interiors. At one end of the spectrum there would be the white gleaming interior of the (new) starship Enterprise and at the other the dank, dark dripping interiors of the Alien movies. Somewhere in between was Han Solo's Millenium Falcon with loads of wires everywhere. Rex's ship was, he thought, a bit like a cross between the Millenium Falcon and a nuclear submarine. Lots of heavy metal hatches, bolts and thick pipes and naked ducting. Mostly painted grey except where Dennis had been asked to cheer things up a bit with some bright yellow paint Rex had managed to obtain. Rex caught Jonny looking at the thickness of the steel hatch.

'Looks like a nuclear sub,' said Jonny. His uncle worked in the navy and spent months under the sea, strangely much to his aunt's apparent relief.

'Well, she is a bit old but very sturdy. The hull is ten inches of Boride Titanium Nano-Combe. Not like all those star-ships made of tin-foil that you see these days.' Rex felt that to save money modern spaceships these days were all force fields and no substance. They passed through the hatch and into the engine room.

Chapter Nine

Chapter Ten

Panos was a tailed Tremote and a brilliant engineer. It is generally agreed by most ape-like races in the Galaxy that they made a pretty smart evolutionary move coming down from the trees. For Tremotes with ravenous Tusked Ground Hogs as their neighbours staying high in the rainforest canopy was the best option. Whereas most humanoids lost their tails in the evolutionary process, Tremotes kept theirs and swung from the trees whilst teasing the Ground Hogs with stupid songs and bombarding them with spiky Java fruit. Even 75 million years later Tremotes and Tusked Hogs prefer to vacation in different locations. Anyway, for the last 20,000 years '1001 uses for your tail' has remained in the (Tremote) best seller lists. Later relevant to our story are use #375 'cunningly holding a laser blaster behind your back whilst surrendering with your hands up', #487 'covering your eyes when you're scared', #621 'playing tennis with two racquets' and we don't need to concern ourselves with #827 'not needing to wash your hands after visiting the washroom'.

Panos put down the badly written manual she was holding with her tail (use #127) and finished re-connecting the stolen Causal Flux Generator to the power supply with the power wrench. This time she had used extra-large bolts and clamps to hold everything in place. Rex and Jonny entered though the hatch. Jonny stared at Panos's tail. Panos was incredibly attractive, in a feline kind of way, but she surprisingly had a tail.

'I don't know where you stole this crazy machine from but it was clearly designed by a madman.' she said without looking up. 'The vibrations it created last time almost shook it out of its mounting. One of the power lines came loose as well.' She had been fixing it for the last two days whilst Rex lay on the beach.

'I can confirm it was built by a madman. It's not stolen. He is kind of lending it to us,' replied Rex. 'It's rude to stare at a Tremote's tail,' he winked at Jonny.

'Sorry,' said Jonny. 'I didn't mean to. It's just ...'

'Who's this charming young man?' Panos smiled, nodding towards Jonny.

'Jonny. He wanted to see the inside of a spaceship. Also, he is a good surfer ...' this time he winked at Panos.

Chapter Eleven

Jonny followed Rex towards the flight deck. 'Hi kid. How do you fancy doing a little surf tournament for me?' Rex started the sales pitch. 'I was really looking forward to it and with this poorly foot... well I am kind of out of action ... you know? Doc Dennis says for the next couple of weeks.'

Johnny was a good surfer and probably the best at his school in St. Ives. This sounded interesting. An interstellar surf tournament. Sounded really cool in fact. Who would guess such things existed?

'Thing is I've paid the entry. Was quite expensive and non-refundable. But hey, you might enjoy it.' Rex had been reading the competition's small print praying for a loop-hole and his prayers had been answered. Clause 133 sub-section 15A. 'There's a sub-clause in the rules that if you are injured and have a Doctor's note you can sub for someone for one of the early rounds. Bit like giving a note to the teacher to miss a day off school.'

'Sounds cool. Early round of what?' Jonny asked.

Rex realised he was saying too much too early. Had to get the kid motivated first. Then subliminally drip more information in slowly.

'Oh ... nothing really. I'm in some kind of amateur intergalactic multi-sports event. Keeps you fit and healthy. That's how I injured my foot. Slipped on the ice you know ...' He paused. Time for a few more positive aspects. Motivational lying came easy to Rex. It was often needed on the crew. 'You will really enjoy it. Could make a name for yourself and become known on the circuit. Might get a medal.'

That last bit sounded good thought Rex. No point in telling the boy it was part of a galactic extreme sports tournament where 80% of the competitors would be stretchered off. A mad competition designed by madmen for the bored masses on their sofas across the Spiral Rim.

The medal sounded good. 'Yea sure. I'll give it a try.'

'That's the spirit. I'll be able to get you home for teatime.' The kid sounded confident thought Rex. Maybe kids have no fear? He remembered seeing a kids' freestyle ski jump competition on Summit once. They could all do somersaults, airborne twists and what not with ease. They actually seemed to enjoy it although just looking at them had made Rex's spine hurt. Maybe the kid was in with a chance. He would tell Panos to keep her mouth shut about the Omega Tiger Sharks. Dennis could deal with them. That was cheating a bit but who cared when you owed a dodgy ancient Egyptian five billion Andurian dollars.

Chapter Twelve

As spaceships went Jonny found the Centennial Eagle pretty cool. Okay, it did not have many of the things he expected of a spaceship such as a transporter room, a shiny flight deck, hundreds of uniformed Federation officers and doors that talked soothingly to you as they slid back and forth. However, it did have a pretty alien called Panos and a friendly robot called Dennis and lots of interesting stuff lying around that Rex had procured from across the Galaxy. He did not know if Rex was an alien for that matter. He looked too human to Jonny so did not qualify.

There were three sleeping cabins on-board as far as he could make out. One was full of Rex's junk, so Dennis had told him he had to share one with Panos. Rex never liked anybody in his cabin and even Dennis was not allowed in there to tidy up the dirty clothes, books, papers, holo discs and empty coffee cups and pizza boxes that Jonny had seen lying around. In Rex's case a stateroom really meant a state Jonny thought.

There was a lounge with comfy chairs and large holo-screens, a dining area and best of all a flight deck. Now this was not the large flashy flight deck of the starship Enterprise but more like the cramped cockpit of a 747 jet that Jonny had once seen on a flight to New York with his dad. A huge number of switches, controls, holo-screens and cool leather looking seats filled the room.

'It's a bit primitive and old fashioned,' remarked Dennis. 'In fact, the control panels are now collectors' pieces. But Sir Rex had it renovated a few years ago with all the latest photonic-nanotronics. He decided to keep all the switches and panels since it has a better visual effect, he tells me.' He recorded that the visual effect did have an effect on Jonny who's pupils instantly dilated by 22%. Maybe Rex was correct and it was not just for impressing girls as Dennis had previously suspected. 'In fact,' he continued, 'most of these controls and switches don't actually do anything. I can fly the ship remotely and completely bypass the controls.'

'What you don't even have to plug in or anything?' asked Jonny who had visions of R2D2 pushing a probe into the Death Star control system.

'No on Earth it would be known as wireless technology, or Bluetooth in your era,' explained Dennis. He was a very patient robot. He had to be with Rex as his master.

Dennis explained the Centennial Eagle was an old Vegan freighter previously used for ferrying all sorts of merchandise around the Galactic Rim. Rex owned it quite some time and kept on updating it with bits he found from around the place. Mostly from space-port bins thought Dennis but he kept this thought to himself. He had been programmed with a prime duty to present his master in the best possible light or at least not in a totally derogatory manner.

'His latest toy is a Causal Flux Generator. He borrowed it from Professor Mitchell. Luckily the ship is pretty sturdy since there is a vibration problem I can't diagnose yet.'

'A what?' asked Jonny. It sounded interesting.

'A time machine to you. In fact, not only are we almost 500 light years distance from our destination but we are also going to arrive almost 50 years before the competition. So, we will have to make a causal displacement on our arrival. Our proper reference frame must regain our original spacetime trajectory. Some of my circuits are still computing the exact displacement coordinates.'

Unlike most people Jonny did not look confused. It was pretty standard stuff – he had seen time travel a hundred times on TV already. Dennis registered a 0% pupil dilation and was slightly confused himself.

Chapter Thirteen

The sports betting companies had taken a real hammering on the Nexus event. The viewers of the Extreme X Cup were often compulsive gamblers. Five competitors had been eaten by Ice Leopards. An unusually high number thought Rex. Usually, it was one or two. It had been apparently a tough winter on Nexus, which had made the Ice Leopards particularly hungry and bad tempered, and it seemed the Blue-Goo competitors had proved particularly tasty. That was the problem with betting on low, poorly defined statistics. The sports betting companies should know better but he had no pity for those blood suckers – even though he was a frequent user of their betting sites.

The next event on Omega he was not looking forward to. For starters he had ripped his foot off on Nexus and the regeneration was not yet completed. He wondered if some Ice Leopard had found his foot – a gourmet snack lying on the piste? He had blacked out when he crashed but was going so fast that he had crossed the finishing line unconscious and miraculously in a good enough time to qualify. Dennis had told him that this was statistically improbable, 'less than 1 in 10 to the minus 5 or thereabouts Sir Rex.' Somehow he had got lucky.

The second problem (and Rex did not want to admit this in public) was that he was scared of water, especially water with waves, and was a pretty awful swimmer. He was okay for a 100 yard paddle across calm St. Ives harbour but the Gravity Waves of Omega V were a different matter. Terrifyingly big waves Rex found, well, terrifying. And then there was the matter of the Omegan Tiger Sharks. Still, he had a solution in the back of his mind – the kid.

Rama came on the holo-screen in Rex's tiny cabin. He was wearing authentic Egyptian robes and seemed in a good mood. Rex could have done without this conversation. To his dismay, Dennis had managed to smugly configure the Flux Generator to capture all forms of intertemporal junk mail, hotel bills and stressful calls from crazy Egyptians.

'Hey Rexy, how's it going? Did you find my scroll in the Brit Museum?' Rex waved the cardboard tube in front of the camera. 'Always amazes me how a bunch of northern barbarian savages could end up having my scroll in their poxy museum. That Professor Mitchell was THE man for time travel I told you.'

Rex thought it was not unsurprising the ancient Egyptian Empire had gone into terminal decline thousands of years ago with Rama's family running things. Sure he ran a fairly decent hotel but an entire empire? Rex found that difficult to imagine.

'Yea sure was easy peasy,' answered Rex trying to be as relaxed as possible in front of a friendly, raving psychopath with undiagnosed megalomaniac tendencies. Early 21st century British Museum guards, with wooden batons and flashlights had not provided much resistance to the latest Vegan neuro knockout gas. 'How's the hotel business? Still keeping the five stars?' Rex taunted. He knew about the impending visit of Outer Rim Michellin hotel inspectors.

Rama looked a bit vexed 'Yes whatever. Same high standards for the last 3000 years.' He quickly changed the subject. 'You had better get going to the next event. Don't let me down,' he looked at Rex's foot, 'and no excuses. You got lucky last time. Very lucky'

'I've got it covered. No problem. See you there. Gotta go.' Jonny was at the door so Rex quickly switched off the holo-screen.

Chapter Fourteen

It was a big changeover day on the planet Thebes, the school vacation had started early in many planetary systems. Shuttles and starships arrived at the Mega Hillton spaceport delivering families like hordes of foreign invaders.

Many were staying at Rama's pride and joy, the luxurious five-star Karnak Hotel and Casino but others, particularly the budget travellers, were quickly transferred on air-coaches to all-inclusive hotels on the other parts of the planet. Rama tried to avoid visiting these cheap, nasty hotels since they disturbed his 'refined' senses. Packed pools, buffet restaurants and overweight sunburnt riff-raff were not Rama's cup of tea.

He stood at the entrance of the Karnak hotel reception in his finest Egyptian regalia; robes made from the finest Theban cotton, a golden necklace and crown inlaid with blue and green semi-precious stones. Everything possible was done to make it seem like genuine ancient Egypt for the millions of annual visitors. They had to compete for tourists against nearby Intergalactic Hotel's Cartoon Planet and Mariott Wild West World which were both pretty shabby and down-market in his opinion. The sector's other Hillton franchise, Paris Planet Hillton, containing over 200 fake Eiffel towers, was his major rival, particularly in quality of service, but the unreliable weather there did not beat the 550 days a year sunshine of Thebes.

Rama always made the effort to look the part and he wished his visitors did the same. Some looked well-dressed but the vast majority of the rabble made his beautiful hotel look an eyesore with their holiday T-shirts, shabby training shoes and kids with ice-cream all over their faces. Now he was only the General Manager but soon, when Rex had completed his mission, he would be more than that. If his plan worked, he would soon have Hoth, his family's ancestral aid, and he would be able to impose strict Pharonic rule over these pathetic tourists. No more smiley Mr. Nice Guy. There would be a strict dress code, no walking on the grass and dramatic wage cuts for all his lazy hotel staff. He would be rich and powerful and a Pharaoh as he deserved to be. It was his genetic birthright after all.

'Excuze me Mr. Ramesses.' Rama was awoken from his megalomaniacal slumber. From millennia of habit, he quickly forced a welcoming smile on his face. An extraordinarily obese Habsburgian tourist with an upside-down map was addressing him.

'Yes, how can I help you Sir?' replied Rama. Soon he would feed hopeless individuals such as this to his crocodiles – although they probably preferred more meat and less lard.

'Izz zee Pharaoh vaterpark zat vay or zat vay?' enquired the tourist innocently.

'Let me point you in the right direction to the waterpark Sir.' Reality had better change soon Rama thought. He had been waiting for over 3000 years and was getting rather impatient.

Chapter Fifteen

The Centennial Eagle left Earth orbit and Dennis engaged the hyperdrive. Unlike Rex he always kept the holo-cloaking device on when flying around on un-contacted planets. That was official Federation protocol. Earth was officially in the Galactic Register as un-contacted for the next few hundred years. Only a few annoyed seagulls blown off course would notice their departure from St. Ives. Rex always liked to leave the cloaking device off. He felt that seeing a monstrous ugly star-freighter the size of a nuclear submarine flying through the sky would give primitive peoples something to talk about around their campfires. He felt it would inspire the natives into creative cave-paintings or maybe new religions. To enhance the traumatising effect, he had Dennis recently paint some terrifying jaws and fangs onto the front of the ship in luminous plasma paint.

Twenty minutes and a cup of coffee later they fell out of hyperspace and into empty space.

'No sign of Omega?' Rex quizzed Dennis.

'No Sir we are about 50 years too early. The planet is not here yet. I will engage the Causal Flux Generator.'

'Brace yourself guys. The rodeo is going to start' said Rex. Selfishly he put his earplugs in and hoped Dennis had done his calculations correctly. He did not want to displace into the middle of a passing planet or something. He was comforted by the thought that at least he had packaged all his remaining Vegan china away this time. Panos put her tail over her eyes and Jonny cautiously fastened his seat belt.

Down in the engine room the blue flame in the Causal Flux Generator began to flicker. It grew in intensity and the spidery filaments around it began to glow and scintillate. The ship's lights suddenly dimmed as the flame shone like a small star drawing all the excess power from the ship's power supply.

Then the shaking started. Slowly at first but then the tremors grew as if the ship were experiencing the start of an earthquake. The flight deck shook and the stars outside the view port windows began to oscillate rapidly back and forth until they became blurred lines. The shaking increased and Jonny gripped his chair to avoid being thrown off. He had a seatbelt on but this was like some sort of rollercoaster ride. Rex tried to think of something nice and pleasurable maybe a whirl-bath or a Sirus Mega cocktail or lying in the sun under some palms but he could not decide.

After a few seconds, but what seemed like an eternity, the shaking stopped. Rex's focus gradually returned and he looked around the cabin. Coffee cups on the floor, a couple of holo-screens annoyingly cracked but otherwise everything looked okay. Luckily Dennis was certified earthquake proof.

'Damage report Dennis?'

'Outer hull integrity OK. Power systems OK. Minor damage to some components but we have spares. We have arrived Sir Rex.'

'Wow look at that! Well cool!" exclaimed Jonny at the view.

'Great another waterworld,' muttered Rex to himself.

Rex looked out the viewscreen. Below in the darkness of space lay a blue iridescent planet with a few high-altitude clouds but otherwise one massive ocean. A waterworld thought Rex. He hated them. Luckily someone had had some sense to put in a few beaches in all that boring water. He could just make out some thin terra-formed sandy crescents seemingly distributed here and there across the ocean. The competition brochure had mentioned that the resort islands were optimally positioned to provide both calm, lagoon like beaches and also the known Galaxy's best wild surf beaches.

Why anybody would want to visit anything but the lagoon-side Rex could not understand.

The Gravity Waves of Omega V were legendary. According to the brochure the tidal forces of Omega's three moons, the strong ocean winds, variable gravity and the spectacular reefs all combined to provide 'awesome' waves. Terrifying rather than awesome thought Rex. Often waves could attain over one mile in height and unless precautions were taken sometimes entire hotel complexes were swept away in a bad storm. The kid had better be a good surfer.

Through the viewport Rex could see hundreds of spacecraft swirling and manoeuvring round the planet in low orbit. He counted at least three gigantic liners from Megastar Galactic Lines jostling for a better view of the islands far below. A few sleek star-yachts were close by. He recognised the banker Lazard Bond's new golden star-yacht the 'Golden Deal', with all its totally unnecessary ostentatious fins, ducts and intakes.

'Totally tasteless,' Rex muttered somewhat jealously. Lazard Bond, so-called King of Galactic 'Junk-Bonds' (as Galactic Time magazine had celebrated on a recent front cover) was a no good, selfish financier. His celebrated activity was to buy or takeover perfectly good, unsuspecting companies and sometimes entire planets by borrowing huge amounts of money from gullible investors. Whole planetary economies were leveraged up to the eyeballs with gazillions in debt and so-called galactic junk bonds. Usually, he managed to pay himself and his friends large profits or dividends before the planets went financially bust, driving their populations into abject poverty. Rex disliked him intensely since he was sure Bond and the others had stitched him up in the Big Table poker game. Bond's vessel was hanging out close to some very ugly, metallic ships sprouting pipes and tanks. They looked like Vegan mining rigs and Rex wondered what they were doing here.

Still the only good thing about being in the competition was the free landing permit. With so many spectators landing was strictly restricted to competitors, sponsors and media. The thought that Lazard Bond would probably have to get the shuttle like everyone else cheered him up a bit. He did not want Dennis to remind him that Lazard Bond could probably afford a personal matter transporter aboard his ship.

Most of Omega was designated a nature reserve. Eco tourism was now the big thing as tourists flocked to see the myriad of spectacular reefs around the islands. Rex thought this was ironic since the Vegan mining company mineral extraction programme had wiped out most of the planet's wildlife a few hundred years ago. The reefs were now virtually 100% artificial with cloned fish and bio-nano engineered coral reefs. His guidebook indicated three notable original surviving species – the microscopic Omegan Seahorse, the Omegan Sea Turtle and the renowned Omegan Tiger Shark whose population had at one point fallen below 20 despite surviving on a favourite diet of plentiful Sea Turtle. Omegan Sea Turtles were a hit with the kids. He remembered he had a poster of one on his bedroom wall when he was younger. Sweet little things with six flippers and bejewelled indigo coloured shells, that you could now ride for 20 dollars an hour. It was a dull article but he read a bit further; 'No Omega Tiger Shark can resist a wholesome snack on the delicious flesh of an Omegan Sea Turtle...' He has a brainwave, one of those flashes of inspiration only he thought he was capable of. Dennis would become a shoal of sea turtles and protect Jonny. Are sea turtles shoals? He didn't know but thought it was a good idea anyway.

Chapter Sixteen

Rex hopped into the Omega VIP enclosure stylishly arranged amongst the beach dunes. Usually, the VIP grub was much better and the alcohol was free. Being a competitor, he could get past the burly security droids with his pass. The downside was that he would have to mix with all the Outer Rim's fashionista and minor celebrities. Later, in the tournament, the minor celebs would be replaced by more serious heavy-weight politicians, royalty and commissioners but for now he had to make do with fairly unknown long-haired musicians, pretentious blond 'It' girls and drunken business men on company junkets. The twins with the spiky hair from the Galactic X Factor were there and Venusian Logora the aristocratic party girl. Passing through the enclosure he noticed Rama deep in conversation with Lazard Bond and Blofield Blatus, the Chair of the Extreme X Cup Organising Committee (EXCOC). Rex knew that each year Rama, to ingratiate himself and have a seat on the Committee, gave a freebie presidential suite to Blatus at his hotel for all his extended family.

Rama was feeling rather pleased with himself. He had just learnt that Blatus had received from the Omegan Prime Minister an extremely lucrative present. In exchange for awarding the second round of the Cup to Omega, Blatus had secretly been provided full mineral extraction rights for the next 1000 years. Blatus, with a suitably large bribe, had just managed to have the nature reserve status of the planet revoked by the Federal Parks Commission. To the horror of the local population, the Vegan mining ships would start pillaging the planet's resources in six weeks time. By extraordinary coincidence, the Prime Minister was also retiring and fortunately his new 'friends' had provided him a leaving gift of a beachside villa, near Blatus's own, on unspoiled Tahyos. He would not need to see those ugly mining ships with their snouts in the Omegan sea. Rama was pleased since although he had no current financial interest in the deal, once he had his hands on the Statue of Hoth the deal would soon belong to him. He would ship all the remaining Omegan Sharks and Sea Turtles back to the aquarium he was planning back on Thebes – or some of lucky ones anyway.

Much to his displeasure his idle power-crazed thoughts were interrupted by the vision of Rex stumbling across the room holding a Sirus Mega cocktail. Rama glared at him.

'What are you doing here? Why aren't you out there competing?' he snarled.

'Look at the foot man. No can do. Got a Doctor's note,' Rex casually replied waving his plastered foot in the air. I have a ringer anyway. It's allowed in the rules.'

'Who is mad enough to compete for you?'

'A lad from Earth. Jonny. Very good surfer by all accounts.'

'Was a good surfer probably. You had better know what you're doing Rex. Whatever happens you are going to Hoth for me. I want my inheritance back.'

There he was moaning about his bloody inheritance again thought Rex. Before Rama could berate him any further Lazard Bond interrupted.

'Hi Rex. How's my robot doing?' leered Lazard. He looked visibly less pissed-off about losing his shiny new robot to Rex in a poker match held a few months ago. At the time he was hopping mad and it was said he immediately decided to randomly fire 10% of his employees to make himself feel better. Obviously, business was looking up or he had recently pillaged the finances of some unfortunate, unsuspecting planet.

'Yea Dennis. Makes a pretty good cup of tea ... and hasn't crashed the ship yet,' joked Rex. To say he disliked Lazard and his dodgy dealings was an understatement.

'Well he is the latest in droid technology. Take good care of him. Cost the company, and me, a small fortune in R&D. See you again soon at the Big Table maybe?' He smirked kind of knowingly. 'Come on Rama it's gonna start,' he grabbed Rama's arm and pushed him towards their private box.

Rex doubted he would ever play at the Billionaires Poker Table, or 'Big Table' as it was known, at Rama's casino again. It was there he had inadvertently lost the huge sum of money he had borrowed from Rama. He still couldn't understand how both his skill and luck had run out that night. It had all happened at such bewildering speed ... all the cards had gone against him in a spectacular fashion.

Chapter Seventeen

Jonny stood on Valhalla beach holding his surf board and looked at the huge waves crashing against the shore. Next to him clustered a small group of six finned Omegan Sea Turtles.

'Some of the largest waves in this sector of the Galaxy,' muttered the turtles. 'Many of them are over one mile high out there.'

'Any advice?' asked Jonny. He wasn't really scared. A wave was a wave as far as he was concerned. At least there was no rocks lying around and the water was warm. Not like Cornwall, where the freezing winter storms brought the biggest and best waves.

The turtles thought for a moment, shuffled around a bit, then answered. 'The highest survival rate is achieved by controlling your fall down the face of the wave.'

'Obvious,' answered Jonny.

'Don't lose balance and fall head first. It's like falling off a high building. It is best to descend slowly then surf the tube or tunnel.'

'Big tube,' Jonny said looking at another of the competitors disappear into one as the huge wave arched over him. It looked great. Jonny was eager to give it a go.

'Yes. Undoubtedly the biggest tube you have ever surfed.'

Dennis did not mind impersonating biological entities. In fact, he quite enjoyed the challenge. Turtles were relatively easy compared with humans. Anyway, Omegan Tiger Sharks had bad eyesight. He had lots of stored data he had decompressed on Omegan Turtles. Many academics had spent many months arduously working on the beaches of Omega V to study the habits of Omegan Turtles. More Federal research grants were spent on the subject than virtually any other species. The Sexy Doppelganger Sirens of Iona were, for some reason, a notable exception. In any case he was not sure he could get the exact shade of indigo shell and so shifted the colour scheme every few minutes to see what looked better. However, he had calculated that a 300,000 Volt shock at precisely 313 Mega-Hertz frequency was entirely sufficient to disrupt an Omegan Shark's nervous system.

Jonny was halfway through the draw. Several competitors had already surfed the wave. Most were pretty hopeless Jonny thought. The unfortunate few had tumbled from the top of the wave. A fall of a few hundred yards meant they had to be carted off by the Medic droids. They looked in a pretty bad state. If you fell nobody tried to swim for shore – the waves were simply too big.

Elmer Diablilo was very good he scored 9 out of 10. Rex had warned Jonny about him. He made it look all too easy. An amazingly cool competitor Jonny thought. Diablilo had found it amusing that Rex had entered Jonny instead.

'Where is that lucky yellow livered chicken?' he had mocked.

Although Diablilo seemed fairly normal some of the competitors were completely bizarre. Jonny had never seen anything like it. It was one thing seeing fake plastic aliens on TV back home but seeing them in the real flesh was something else. It would take a bit of getting used to. The huge scaly Mega-Troll was actually terrifying and the bug-eyed Callistan Mudskipper friendly but unfeasibly slimy. He wondered if it was unfair that the strange, remaining Blue-Goo could just stick to his surfboard? And did he even need to breath? And how could he paddle with no arms?

The Marshall ran along the beach and told Jonny to get ready. The sea turtles slipped into the water and the droid jet-ski arrived. Everybody was towed out to the backside of the waves since the waves were too big to paddle over or through them. Jonny gave the thumbs up to the Marshall and the droid set off. Jonny hung on for dear life as the droid bounced over the smaller waves and plotted a course around the big rollers. 'Here goes,' thought Jonny. He glanced around, a flock of flying camera droids from different news and sports channels followed him, all jostling for the best camera angles.

Chapter Eighteen

Rex was slumped in the corner of the VIP lounge. He had consumed moderately, a couple of Sirus Mega cocktails, and had tried chatting up a few 'It' girls but he could not take his mind off the event. It was not like him to feel any conscience but he did feel ever so slightly guilty luring a poor kid into a dangerous competition. He looked at the holo-screen it was Jonny's turn.

'Today folks we have our first substitute of the tournament. Rex Rogers lost a foot on Nexus and graciously provided a tasty hors d'oeuvre for the Ice Leopards. For the Gravity Wave Event we have representing him Jonny Jenson – a young kid from Cornwall, Earth. Never heard of Earth? Nor have we. Well, in fact he is the only Earth guy ever to compete in the Extreme X Cup.'

'Well maybe he will put Earth on the map. We wish him luck, Dec.'

Toujours nauseous the commentary thought Rex. The kid was reaching the drop off zone on a large roller. The droid released him. Suddenly one of the camera droids picked up something interesting, a large fin the size of a double decker bus a few hundred yards away.

'Wow Ant. Look at that it's our first Omega Shark of the day.'

'Looks huge Dec! Must be a hungry chap by the speed he is moving at,' the commentators sprung into life. Jonny's potential misfortune was going to give them something exciting to talk about. Covering momentous and hopefully tragic events was what they wished for every morning on their way to work.

Suddenly the conversation became very animated as if all the news teams had been waiting all day for this moment. In fact on virtually all channels across the Spiral Rim programs were interrupted to bring live footage of the excitement. Old news reels of shark attacks were shown, meaningless statistics were quoted and the hype started to bring the moment to fever pitch. A live feast was about to happen.

Rex anxiously ran outside and looked at the real wave from the top of the beach. He hoped turtle Dennis could provide convincing shark bait.

Chapter Nineteen

The droid had dropped Jonny near the top of a very large wave. Very clever thought Jonny, he had almost the exact velocity to match the wave. He paddled a few strokes and passed over the waves crest. He then carefully stood up on the board. Looking down he felt dizzy – it was a long way down. The roar of the wave was deafening. He careered, staying low, down the face of the wave then flipped the board to float effortlessly across the cliff high wall of clear blue water. It was the biggest, most powerful wave Jonny had ever surfed and he felt great! The adrenaline pumped though him and he tried to remain focused and relaxed. The enormous wave passed over his head to enclose him in the tube. A gaggle of camera droids accelerated after him – he was going very fast. Glancing over his shoulder he saw a large fin approaching. What the hell was that? It was some sort of shark maybe? And moving very fast. How could a shark be that big though? He crouched lower and angled further down the wave to accelerate. The fin seemed to be closing on him then suddenly pulled back. It had given up. He had outrun it. A few seconds later he exited the tunnel. The pick-up droid was waiting. He grabbed it and made for the beach.

Rex was there waiting. He was jumping up and down enthusiastically. A large crowd of cheering supporters, news crew and Marshalls had formed.

'You scored a perfect 10 Jonny! Judges unanimous. Perfect surf and you outran an Omega Shark. Nobody ever done that before and kept all their legs,' Rex winked.

Chapter Twenty

It was a week before the next tournament and Rex wanted to explore a cunning plan he had concocted to erase his gambling debts. He had a time machine after all – why not use it? A short cut to fame and fortune. He would settle for the latter. He needed to first ask the Professor a few questions.

The Professor was still asleep at his bench when they arrived back in Vigilstrammer two weeks earlier and 50 light years distant. Rex shook him awake. The professor had a terrific hangover. Rex plied him with his favourite antidote he had brought in a flask: a Nebula Headoxidiser, a potent cocktail of inedible eggs well past their sell-by date, yellow tomatoes, heavy duty Theban spices and a quadruple shot of Ruskovan vodka. Based on experience he found it highly effective and it was far more fun than those anti-hangover tablets you could buy everywhere. The mildly hallucinogenic spices always put the recipient in a great mood as well which was a major plus in a situation like this.

'Wow that was a great night out!' exclaimed the Professor. 'I'd like to do it more often but my heart would probably give out.'

He looked a bit green round the gills but Rex thought he would be okay. The Professor looked at Jonny through his half open eyes.

'Hi, I'm Jonny,' Jonny waved at the Professor but he was pretty unresponsive in this state.

The Professor gazed past Jonny and saw that the Flux Generator was missing.

'They've taken it!' he gasped, suddenly straightening himself. He looked very worried despite the normally cheery effect of the Theban spices.

'No Professor. I took it for safekeeping. It works just fine,' said Rex. More than half of what he just said was a lie.

'You mean you used it?' the Professor looked bewildered but truly amazed.

'Sure, we did a little trip back to Earth circa 21st century local time. About 50 years backwards. There is a nice little museum I found which ...' The Professor interrupted him.

'You went yourself?' Rex nodded. 'You are a very brave man. You see I've only ever tried it on my Hiberian hamsters. Displacements of a couple of minutes that's all.'

Rex looked worried and felt a bit nauseous. This was news to him. He thought it was finished, commissioned or what not. He didn't know it was experimental. Dennis had told him it looked okay – but then again Dennis only read the theory papers. He could have been blown to pieces or de-quantised or whatever across both time and space.

'But the manual seemed to suggest it was finished and tested?' he pondered.

'Grant applications my dear boy. You have to exaggerate to get research funding. Extrapolate things forward to get your hands on grant money. Everybody does it.'

'Anyway, it worked fine. Some of my best china got broken though.'

There was a loud banging at the cafe door upstairs.

'What's that noise?' said Jonny peering up the staircase.

Rex realised he had stupidly left the cafe door open. He ran to the top of the stairs and peered round. Two large figures were in the doorway. He recognised those shadows; undoubtedly the Chrono Police. They had followed him somehow.

'Chrono Police,' he said to the Professor. 'Is there another way out?' He slammed the steel door at the bottom of the staircase and firmly bolted it.

'Don't worry the chocolate should distract them for a while,' said the Professor calmly. 'There is a hidden way out the back.' He started to fill a large holdall with various papers, calculations and gadgets. There was a vast amount of stuff and the bag looked far too small but somehow it all fitted.

'It all needs to come with us I'm afraid. Can't let them get their hands on all my research. And especially not these two intrepid chaps of mine.'

He handed Jonny a large cage with two friendly looking hamsters inside. 'Einstein and Eddington,' was the introduction. Jonny had heard about Einstein, he was famous, but not Eddington. How did the Professor know about Earth and Einstein?

'Eddington proved Einstein correct you know,' explained the Professor absent mindedly. 'Although ... everybody else in the Galaxy, except for those still living in caves and knocking rocks together, already knew he was right.' He continued packing.

Rex had forgotten about the chocolate shop. After the success with the Milka bars he had discovered that some species, notably the Viregi and Centaurians found chocolate irresistible. The mere whiff of it was enough to send them crazy. They were total addicts. Their neuronic pleasure centres were saturated by the smell and taste of cocoa to such an extent that on Centauri chocolate was a banned substance and deemed an illegal narcotic. There were squeals of joy upstairs as the Chrono police discovered about half a ton of the finest quality Vigilstrammer chocolate.

They ran out the back and down the alley to where Rex had illegally and very antisocially parked his ship on a children's play area. It was early and he thought it would disturb nobody but some kids were already kicking a football against the hull of the ship.

'You can't park here mate. You'll get a ticket,' said one of them.

'Your robot looks really stupid too,' said another bouncing his ball off Robbie the Robot's head making his antenna whirl round.

Dennis was not pleased. He was just trying to fix the ship's sub-ether antenna that the kids had bent out of shape. He was wondering if a 300 kilo-Volt shock would clear the kids off – it had worked on the Omegan Tiger Shark. 'Here you go boys,' said the Professor as he offered a large box of shiny, wrapped kids chocolates that he had somehow produced from his holdall. The kids looked pleased.

'Great thanks granddad!' They laughed and ran off to the other end of the playground blowing raspberries at Rex.

Rex breathed a sigh of relief. He had just been wondering if he had any of that Vegan neuro knockout gas left over. Generally, Rex disliked kids although Jonny was growing on him.

'I take it you don't have grandchildren?' observed the Professor as he climbed through the open hatch. He wanted to see how his causal violation device worked in practice. He had been trying to find some life-form with extended consciousness, other than his hamsters, to test it on for some time but had not found any insane volunteers – up to now that was.

Chapter Twenty-one

Rex was eager to ask the Professor lots of questions. Perhaps he could help Panos and Dennis fix the vibration problem? But more pressing personal issues came first.

'Why is it again I can't go back and fix that poker game?' enquired Rex. The Professor's previous explanation had lost him completely.

'Causality is a strange thing. We don't know the initial cause or the final cause and effect of the Universe,' the Professor continued. 'Causal connections are closely bound together. You can go back and change some events and not others. Some are intrinsically important to the future development of the Universe. They are the props that keep reality supported in some sense.'

'But I thought that everything was indeterministic. The future undecided.' Rex tried to sound more intelligent but he was out of his depth already. 'Surely that's what quantum mechanics is all about. Uncertainty principle, yes?'

'Yes, well quantum mechanics suggests that in an ideal sense since it is an equilibrium condition. But below the surface things are probably different.'

'What do you mean?' Rex's tenuous grip on physics was being rapidly undermined.

'Well imagine a tree,' said the Professor.

'What kind of tree? Palm? Vegan monkey puzzle? Earth oak?' He liked palm trees best for some reason. He imagined a palm tree.

'An oak is good. The branching of the tree represents different causal paths. The twigs of the tree radiate out in uncertainty and we might be able to change these without altering the tree too much. It will still stand up in the wind and the elements, so to speak.'

The explanation verged on the mystical but Rex was good with that. He found it comforting. He had his doubts about physics anyway.

'But we can't change the thicker branches and certainly not the thick trunk. That could be a disaster. The entire tree of causal connections represents the Universe. In fact, physics, us and everything are emergent from the causal tree or network – the universe of possibilities.'

'Okay so I can go back and change the poker game then?' Rex wanted to get back to the point.

'Maybe, maybe not. In some sense the Universe knows what it is doing. Some causal connections are too well established.' The Professor paused a moment, thinking. 'Perhaps you should try and change something where your past self is not present. Could be safer.'

The Professor was not entirely convinced of his theories and ideally, he needed more empirical evidence to support them. His experiments on his hamsters had led to some confusing and conflicting results. Rex was not convinced either but he knew that (a) causality violation seemed to work – he had stolen Rama's scroll from the British Museum after all, (b) he was in possession of a functioning causality violation device and (c) he owed Rama five billion Andurian dollars and importantly (d) might not survive the next event.

It was worth a shot. Nobody would get hurt. He had abandoned the idea of fixing the Big Table poker game that had got him into all this mess. Based on what the Professor had said he should avoid running into himself in the past. He probably wouldn't like himself anyway he concluded. He got Dennis to program a route back to Nexus for two days before the start of the luge event.

Chapter Twenty-two

Rex arrived, as planned, two days before the luge event and walked confidently into the spaceport betting shop. The Nexan Unlimited Stakes branch notoriously had the most competitive betting odds for the Extreme X tournament. Panos had thought it was a stupid idea but not stupid enough to be persuaded from loaning Rex all her life savings. 'It's a dead cert. A no brainer,' Rex had argued. She wanted at 50% cut though and gave Rex her measly, insubstantial two million Andurian dollars. She had been saving for a retirement tree house in one of the best Tremote forests back home.

The pasty faced Nexan frowned a bit when Rex placed a string of crazy, out of the money bets. Still an idiot was born every second, or probably every millisecond across the Spiral Rim he thought. Low probabilities of winning ... 5 people to be eaten by Ice Leopards 20:1, first death Stefan Schumachen 60:1, 2 Blue-Goos to be eaten 120:1, 63% casualty rate 30:1 and cheekily he thought, Rex Rogers to qualify but be injured. On the latter bet he offered 80:1 although Mr. Rogers had argued that some robot of his had calculated at least 10,000:1. In any case he quoted a combined odds of 4000:1. The house was going to make an easy 2 million Andurian dollars. Rex knew otherwise. He placed the bets and quickly left.

Outside he paused at a realtor. He was going to be rich, seriously rich. There were some expensive looking villas on Tahyos III. Beachfront, pools, maid service. Nice. He would buy one with all the money. Maybe one of those Suncruiser star-yachts as well? He left dreaming. He quickly calculated again to reassure himself; two million dollars at 4000:1 odds would payout eight billion well deserved dollars. If everything went to plan, he would not only clear his name and gambling debts but be up some three billion dollars.

Chapter Twenty-three

They arrived in the Hoth system for round 3 of the Extreme X Cup. It appeared that the Professor had fixed the vibration problem somewhat. He had recalibrated the Causal Flux Generator's quantum field for the size of the ship rather than for a large cage of hamsters. He told Rex that for small time jumps of a few weeks there would be no discernible vibration and he could drink his coffee at the same time.

Rex picked up the latest local sub-ether news. It appeared in the business pages that Nexan Unlimited Stakes betting had unexpectedly gone bust. Immediately after the competition they had filed for Federal bankruptcy protection on the basis of a possible undisclosed large sum payout to an unnamed individual. In the editorial there was some speculation that it was a certain Captain Rex Rogers who had placed the bets but Nexan Unlimited was saying nothing. Nexan Unlimited's parent company, Galactic Index, was distancing itself from its subsidiary on the basis of possible fraud by the Nexan management. Great thought Rex, so much for being 'unlimited'. Now he would have to get a lawyer and spend years going through the Federal courts to get his money.

Chapter Twenty-four

Corruption was rampant across the Galaxy. Despite the formation of the Federation, the rule of law and a voluntarily Constitution adopted by many planets, hard Galactic Credits kept the wheels of commerce turning. A Federation Commission had been formed 5000 years ago to try and organise things better and avoid internecine disputes and squabbles between star-systems degenerating into war. Quickly the Commission had become a bloated corrupt organisation. Numerous investigative holo-documentaries had 'sensationally' revealed how fat Commissioners managed to afford sleek star-yachts, villas on the perfect beaches of Tahyos III and innumerable young, nubile mistresses, invariably from Ruskova V, on their measly civil servant salaries. Rex quite liked it like that. If you had contacts everybody was bribable and everything achievable. A galactic bureaucracy became a gold mine of opportunities if you knew how to exploit it.

Unfortunately for Rex one element of the bureaucracy was totally incorruptible – the FTO or the galactic Federal Tax Office. They were hyper efficient in calculating and raising tax and tireless in tracking down galactic citizens. An entire planet, staffed by enthusiastic clones, was dedicated to querying, checking and chasing up all those unpaid tax bills even those less than the cost of a Federal sub-ethergram. The fact that most of the tax was later squandered on corrupt Federal projects did not distract from the inspectors' almost religious fervour when tracking down tax evaders.

Chapter Twenty-Five

There was a knock or rather a deliberately distracting beep at Rex's cabin door.

'This arrived for you Sir Rex,' Dennis handed Rex a Federal recorded sub-ethergram. Not another bill thought Rex. It made for extremely bad reading – at least for the tax payer. Rex had to sit down and reached for his bottle of vintage Ecossian whisky. He needed a strong drink to calm his nerves.

'Mr. R. Rogers. We have completed your tax assessment for the Federal Financial Year 5011–5012 and have discovered that you have overlooked to pay your Federal Property Gains tax for your villa on Tahyos III. From our records you purchased the villa in 5001 and sold in 5011. We calculate that you owe the Federal Tax Office AD 7,9991,736.11. We hope that this is an error or oversight on your part. You have 21 days to pay the outstanding amount. We politely remind you that the FTO has the power to acquire personal assets and impound spacecraft on non-payment. Yours sincerely, Claudia Widecombe, FTO Deputy Controller.'

Weird. Somehow changing the past had interfered with the even more distant past. How had that happened? The Professor had not mentioned that. He was no better off than before – assuming he would get any money out of Nexan Unlimited betting. Very depressingly the Universe was conspiring against him. The whole thing was made even worse in that he could not even remember having or enjoying a villa on Tahyos. At least he should remember a few pool parties but no this new past had not even pervaded his consciousness. Perhaps it was a mistake by the FTO. But they were renowned for never making mistakes. Anyway, they had efficiently attached a holo-image of the lovely villa with Rex standing outside it smiling. There was a large infinity pool in an exotic garden with steps down to the white sand beach.

Panos was mad with Rex for losing her savings. Rex promised to recuperate all her money and, in the meantime, she could have what was left of his prized Vegan china collection. Panos annoyed went round the ship looking for anything else of value. The Professor looked amazed when Rex explained. He described it as an example of 'causal conservation' – one event had cancelled out another to preserve the future. The winnings on the bet he had made had been cancelled out by the unexpected tax bill almost exactly to within four significant figures. There was probably a prize-winning physics paper in there somewhere, but unfortunately one empirical observation did not provide a theory. He felt that Rex was probably meant to continue the Extreme X Cup and compete for Rama. There was no easy way out. Rex did not believe in Fate but started to feel Destiny, with a capital 'D', was staring him in the face.

Chapter Twenty-Six

Orchidia had been a flowering, democratic planet. Its people were happy, cultured and artistic. For 5000 years it had produced some of the Galaxy's most imaginative works of art and critically acclaimed operas. One day 3000 years ago a misrouted trunk arrived at the local spaceport. A disgruntled baggage handler named Smitheson Smiles – possibly the only grumpy person on Orchidia – decided to open it. He later claimed he did not want to open it but the trunk whispered to him. It told him he was the chosen one and was destined for great things. The trunk was marked Egypt, Earth to New Mega Hillton Hotel Project, Tarsus II (Thebes). Strange he had never heard of Egypt or Earth. He had heard of Mega Hillton. They ran crap hotels and he had had a miserable time in one on his honeymoon. The food had been truly awful and the service worse than bad. Smitheson opened the trunk and inside he found something dark – a statuette with stars in its eyes. It told him he would be great and powerful, provided he worshipped It.

Within six months all the inhabitants of Orchidia, bar a select cult of crazy monks led by Smitheson Smiles, had been enslaved and lived in poverty and famine. The beautiful gardens of Orchidia were ripped down and the graceful works of art smashed. The planet was renamed Hoth in the statue's honour. The people of Hoth toiled under the hot, burning sun building futile monuments in praise of the glory of their new deity.

Still the upside Rama thought was the massive unexploited tourist potential of the Spires of Hoth. Now a UFESCO galactic heritage site, thousands of spectacular religious spires stretched many tens of miles up into the planet's ionosphere from the desert plains far below. Of course, no tourists were actually allowed to visit the sacred monuments (the mad monks did not allow it) but they looked good on postcards. Any fat Habsburgian tourist who didn't read the small print in the tourist brochure, saying the monuments were closed until further notice, was captured and sent to work 20 years along with the remaining Orchidean population down the Hoth slave mines – notorious for their great working conditions. Huge tracts of the interior of Hoth were mined by hand, since the monks thought it was more redemptive for wicked souls, to provide raw materials to build the Spires.

Rama was actually very jealous of the Spires of Hoth. The best his ancestors could achieve in a couple of thousand years, even with the statue's help, was the Pyramids of Giza, which were embarrassingly small in comparison. As an excuse, Rama put this down to the enhanced enslavement opportunities offered by modern technology. He was sure he could do even better than the Monks of Hoth.

Chapter Twenty-Seven

Rama had sent him a densite black sack and a shielded metallic casket. The bag itself was heavy, especially with the statue inside. The figurine was black, shiny jackal headed and about one foot high. Rama had had it nano-fabricated somewhere. The replica looked old but was in fact brand new. He had told Rex that once he had performed the switch to ignore what the statue had to say and immediately put it in the densite bag. Rex wondered whether it was really feasible that a statue could have anything intelligent to say. He reluctantly, and perhaps unwisely, did away with the contents of his reserve parachute bag across his chest and stuffed in the densite bag instead.

All the base jumps were going to be made from the Central Spire of Hoth, the tallest and most magnificent of all the pillars that stretched across the Hothian desert. It was said to be so high that the clear blue sky faded into the inky blackness of outer space at the summit. From top to bottom the tower had been meticulously hand engraved in insane religious icons. Rex could make out sphinxes, jackal and baboon headed men, winged beetles and images of mortal men mostly suffering at the hands of the baboons and jackals. Nice creative bit of lunatic artwork thought Rex. He wondered how the slaves had carved the upper reaches of the tower where the atmosphere was thin. Were the slaves given pressure suits or did they have to hold their breath? As he looked, he could see the parachute of one of the competitors open a few hundred feet up and glide off towards the target zone. Several competitors had already jumped and conditions were good. It was Rex's turn next. He exited the airvan and walked towards the base of the spire.

Chapter Twenty-Eight

He liked it at the top of His spire. It had taken them about 1000 years to build for Him but from it He could see across the vastness of space. He had a great view of all He could now conquer. Different planets and peoples awaited Him. He had fulfilled his task on Hoth and now needed to leave this place. The monks and the miserable, wretched population had started to bore Him. He had been here far too long. A huge intellect like His required new creative projects. He sensed someone was coming. Someone who would take Him through those depths of space. He had foreseen this date. Greater things awaited Him. His power would grow ... the entire Galaxy would worship Him!

Chapter Twenty-Nine

Only competitors were allowed on Hoth. Spectators were forbidden to land on the surface and the air was thick with aircoaches, shuttles and camera droids. That was the best deal Rama could negotiate with the Monks of Hoth, despite a large charitable donation to building a new spire and sharing the same regenerative consultant as Smitheson Smiles. Rex noticed that the friendly Marshalls had been replaced by fanatical monks with mad gleams in their eyes. Two of them ushered Rex into a small lift that whisked him to the top of the spire one hundred miles upwards. After what seemed like a very long time in the company of the mute monks the lift opened into a small dark, amphitheatre. The ceiling opened into the clear darkness of space and the seemingly nearby stars shone brightly. Some form of force dome thought Rex. In the centre some 20 yards away was the jackal-headed Statue of Hoth on a plinth. It was guarded by four beefy looking monks nearby. They seemed to be armed with just wooden staffs but looked pretty serious.

One of the monks spoke for the first time. 'This way, Sir, to the jump zone. The starting droid is waiting.'

Rama had explained that he only had a couple of minutes to perform the switch. Rex turned on the pressure suit and simultaneously released the Vegan neuro knockout gas hidden in his belt. The effect was instantaneous as the gas diffused quickly across the room. The monks' eyes glazed over. A few molecules of the neuro gas up anybody's nose and their brain would 'trip' and enter a repetitive cycle of thought. The molecules had been engineered to have a duration of a few minutes after which the unsuspecting subjects would not even know they had been gassed. They would have a nice couple of minutes thinking about their last holiday, how nice Hoth was or how they really had enjoyed making all those citizens suffer, holding their breath, while engraving the spire.

Rex sprang into action. He fished out the electromagnetic pulse disruptor that Rama had sent him. He fired a quick pulse at the plinth of the statue. Apparently, it would temporarily immobilise the alarm systems surrounding the statue. Rex did not know it but He had disabled them anyway. He wanted to escape and move to new worlds. Rex took the statue. It was heavy but about the same weight as the replica. He tried not to look at it but was drawn to its eyes. They glistened and it seemed briefly like there was an infinity of stars inside – a whole universe. 'You have come for me Rex. I can make you great ...' a soothing, suggestive voice whispered in Rex's head.

'Quiet mate. Not interested. Have enough problems. Thanks anyway,' Rex muttered. Another megalomaniac he thought. The statue and Rama would get along great together. He threw the statue in the shielded bag, placed the replica on the plinth and ran to the jump site.

The starting droid was waiting next to the black doorway. Rex did not have time to be scared. Besides there was no water this time. He checked his main chute – it had better work. The hidden statue was now well secured to his chest inside the reserve chute bag.

'3, 2, 1... jump!' the droid announced.

He crossed his fingers and threw himself out of the dark doorway. It was cold and dark outside as he fell in the shadow of the Central Spire. The graceful curvature of Hoth's blue atmosphere dominated the horizon. A few tops of nearby spires were visible a few miles below. Almost 100 miles of free fall awaited him down the face of the spire. He felt as if he were flying across an undulating surface of strange Egyptian gods. His only company in the silence were the camera droids buzzing round him.

Chapter Thirty

The spaceport on Mega Hillton Thebes was surrounded by palm trees, stone sphinxes and innumerable pointed obelisks. The terminal building was a large sandstone structure with huge coloured engravings of hawk-headed gods on the outside. Jonny found it difficult to believe an entire planet could be dedicated to an Egyptian themed holiday resort. Also, everything looked so genuinely old and crumbly. Not plastic and totally fake like the Harry Potter castle Jonny had seen at Disneyland.

'That's because it is actually over 3000 years old,' explained Rex as he lowered the landing ramp, 'and Rama is a real genuine Egyptian. The real deal.'

'How's that possible ... a real Egyptian?' quizzed Jonny.

'Well story has it. In fact, it's in the Mega Hillton brochure. That Rama came from Egypt, Earth and helped design the Mega Hillton. He has worked for them ever since as the General Manager. It's a franchise now of course. Just like his old place except there are burger bars, casinos and it's a bit more hygienic.'

Rama was waiting for them on the landing pad. He looked very pleased with himself. Resplendent in his flowing white gown and blue coloured headgear. He had a great suntan and did not look very old thought Jonny.

'He has the best regenerative consultant money can buy. Looks late 30's but is really pushing over 3000 years old,' Rex whispered jealously. He had only managed to afford knocking a couple of years off a few years back and the rejuvenating effects had worn off.

Rama's name-badge read 'Unhaluum Ramesses. General Manager. Thebes Mega Hillton *****,' and below, 'The Land of the Pharaohs for the Galaxy's Best Family Vacation.'

'Ah Rex. Good to see you. You did well. I am pleased,' Rama spoke with a regal yet business like air. He looked at Jonny. 'And Jonny too. Nice surfing Jonny.'

'No problem Rama,' answered Rex. 'Here it is. Your beloved statue. The debts are cleared, I hope? He tried to briefly offer me cosmic domination but I told him that ain't my gig.' Dennis clanked along behind holding the Statue of Hoth safely sealed in the casket.

'Of course my dear boy. Your little gambling problems have disappeared. I am a man of my word. Amelia my assistant will show you to your suites and I have arranged two million dollars of credits for you at the Palm casino.'

Rex glanced at Amelia with interest. Pretty, bejewelled and Egyptian looking – even though she probably wasn't and the jewels were probably fake as well.

'Max here will take the casket.' A muscled security guard with a large lethal curved scimitar materialised and took the casket containing the statue from Dennis. 'We will have dinner together tomorrow night Rex. We have new interesting, profitable things to discuss.'

'Oh no!' instantaneously flashed up Rex's front cortex. Not new schemes. Rama's ventures were generally highly profitable for Rama but dangerous and marginally profitable (at best) for Rex.

'Enjoy yourselves,' Rama continued. 'Jonny you probably won't find the casino interesting. If you ask Amelia, she can take you to the Pharaoh Waterpark. All the kids love it. The wave machine probably won't be as big as you're used to though.' He laughed and wandered off.

Rama was in a very good mood thought Rex. It was generally wise to keep megalomaniacs happy. He was happy too. His gambling debts were erased, he was in one piece and he could lie by the pool all afternoon and visit the casino in the evening after a nice massage in the spa. All was nearly perfect in the egocentric world of Rex Rogers.

Chapter Thirty-One

'Well, Mr. Ramesses would have been Pharaoh Ramesses XII but things were a bit political in old Egypt. Mega Hillton was looking for a new themes and designers and they approached Mr. Ramesses and realised he was a creative genius.' Amelia continued, 'He designed most of the hotel complex himself you know. His fabrics and prêt-a-porter collection are also well known across the Spiral Rim.'

At least Amelia thought her boss was a genius Rex mused as he left the others and wandered off in the opposite direction towards the pool. Egyptian emperor to hotel manager and dress designer. No wonder Rama was so crazy.

Amelia opened the door to the connected suites. Rex had his own suite and Jonny and Professor Mitchell shared. Panos had stuff to fix on the ship with Dennis. Apparently, they usually played tennis a lot when they were here. Jonny wondered if a tailed Tremote with two racquets versus a clumsy Robby the Robot was a fair match.

Jonny and Professor Mitchell were speechless. Professor Mitchell only got to stay in sordid two star hotels whilst at academic conferences and Jonny had never seen such a big, opulent hotel room. A vast Egyptian themed lounge with comfy sofas, luxurious fabrics and palm crested pillars lead out to a large stone balcony that overlooked a spectacular ornamental lake. Beyond, the gardens lead down to a palm tree fringed river where white sailed feluccas peacefully sailed.

'Wow, well cool! Two bathrooms, mini-robobar, computer games library ...' Jonny enthused. Professor Mitchell flicked through the enormous room service menu written on fake papyrus. There appeared to be whole world out there beyond academia he knew nothing about. What on earth was an 'Ionian Topless Full Body Massage' at 2000 AD? And the

'Authentic Royal Barge Experience' at AD 250? That sounded a bit too exhausting. He would give that a miss.

'Have a good time. If you need anything ring me,' Amelia said. 'Jonny I'll pick you up at two for the waterpark.'

Chapter Thirty-Two

The waterpark had been a good laugh. Amelia had left earlier and Jonny had stayed on to do the Snappy Crocodile Plunge a couple more times. All the kids loved the water slide into a pool of large hungry crocodiles. The crocs could not actually get to you of course because an invisible force screen kept their jaws from biting you at the very last minute. It was thoroughly addictive and made Jonny's adrenaline pump hard. Little did he know that Rama was itching for the day when he could just turn that force screen off and feed his guests to his much loved crocodiles.

On the way back he noticed a couple of hotel technical staff wheeling past large Syrus Droid Foundry crates. Maybe a new themed ride or something was being set up? Jonny wanted to find out so followed the technicians along the path through the palms.

In a clearing he could see a large ornamental building was being completed. Helmeted construction crews and a variety of droids were completing a large portico of pillars and concreting the steps. At least it looked like concrete but was drying instantly to look like ancient marble. From a distance at the edge of the clearing he noticed that the technicians had hauled the crates upright and were opening them. The contents of one had already climbed out – a three metre high hawk-headed robot. It seemed pretty scary and Egyptian he thought and also just like the carvings he had seen on the Spires of Hoth. Looked like a cool new part of the resort. He couldn't wait to tell Rex.

Chapter Thirty-Three

Rex was feeling very relaxed or at least as relaxed as he had felt in a long time. He was planning to drop out of the Extreme X Cup now that he had fulfilled his bargain with Rama. There was no point risking his life any longer for some stupid competition. There were easier and less dangerous ways of making a living. Besides he was feeling rather pleased with himself since he had won good money at a few of the casino gambling tables last night. He would be able to pay Panos back her money and the rest of his winnings would provide some good pocket money for a while.

He had spent most of the day lounging around by the hotel pool, chatting up the girls and drinking various tasty cocktails. He had to admit though that, although he was a bit of a sun worshipper, the broiling Theban sun was a bit severe. His skin was feeling a bit red and raw despite the heavy duty after-sun cream he had applied before leaving the hotel.

He made his way down towards the river in the late afternoon sun. Across the well-tended laws with their luscious thick-bladed grass and through the perfectly coiffured palm grove. He admired their thick trunks that had been precisely clipped by the ever-present team of droid gardeners. Everything was perfect. There was only one minor blot on the horizon and that was dinner with Rama. He never knew what surprises meetings with Rama might bring and so was slightly wary of being talked into some harebrained scheme.

A huge set of marble steps lead down to the landing stage beside the wide river. The large white plinths on either side supported gleamingly polished gilded statues of various pharaohs and sphinxes. Rex sat down on one of the bottom steps and waited. He was a few minutes early for his dinner date with Rama.

The other bank of the river was sandy desert as far as the eye could see. The uninitiated eye might think that it had been left as wilderness or the gardening droids had not terraformed beyond the hotel gardens but the scene was too perfect, too sublime. Rex realised that the various ruins poking out of the sand had been deliberately placed and even the sand dunes had been sculpted to maintain the awesome beauty of the view. Totally synthetic he cynically thought. But hey, he liked it like that. It was entirely safe with no snakes, scorpions or bugs to annoy the hotel visitors. There were probably in that desert even drinks and suntan cream dispensers every couple of hundred yards.

The tranquillity was broken by the sight of Rama's huge barge sailing round the bend in the river. It was, Rex had to admit, fairly amazing. A huge oared wooden galley, with a massive square red sail, painted blue, white and red. Its prow had a huge golden, ornamental battering ram in the shape of a dragon's head and both ends of the boat had huge green and white decorative fins that resembled giant palm leaves. He knew Rama had spent a lot of money on this reproduction royal Pharaoh's barge and was very proud of it. Rama had even decided, in the absence of real slaves, that using droids to row his barge was not authentic enough. He had instituted a compulsory rowing club for the hotel staff to propel his vessel on days when the wind was lacking. Sometimes even hotel guests liked to participate in the 'Authentic Royal Barge Experience', paying AD 250 an hour for the privilege of a historic sweaty workout.

As it approached Rex saw Rama onboard sitting on a large, high backed golden throne. He waved at Rex.

'Hi Rexy. Heard you did well in my casino last night.'

'Yea maybe my luck is back.'

The barge had come to a smooth halt by the quay and a gang-plank was lowered.

'Come aboard my humble vessel,' Rama invited, not bothering to get up from his throne. A smiling Amelia helped Rex aboard.

'Hello Rex. Hope you had a good day. Your nose looks a bit red though,' she said passing him some exotic, fruity looking cocktail.

'Yea misjudged the sun a bit,' he had to admit it.

'Well, there is sun-cream in your hotel welcome pack. Your friend Jonny was a nice boy. We had a great time at the waterpark,' she continued.

Rex had never been to the waterpark and it was no doubt full of horrid screaming kids and families. He had probably made a wise decision to never go there. Besides he didn't like water much and especially when it contained dangerous wild animals like sharks and crocodiles that kids these days seemed to get a kick out of. He followed Amelia to the back of the boat where some waiters were laying up a table with some of Rama's Vegan china and silverware. Dinner for two, it looked very romantic except that the dinner was with Rama.

Rama finally got off his throne and greeted Rex with a hug and a kiss on each of his cheeks. Rex never really liked other men kissing him. It was all a bit too Mediterranean but Rama had had thousands of years of practice and it was pretty painless.

'Good to see you Rex. Tonight Jacques, my chef has a real treat for us.'

'What's on the menu from the great Jacques tonight?' In Rex's experience Egyptians really knew how to entertain and although the combinations sounded pretty weird they always tasted good.

'An hors d'oeuvre of pasties of Lesser Spotted Ocelots tongues imported from Vega – a very rare speciality. Followed by a terrine of wild Antares Mega-Buffalo hooves and then the chef's speciality, grilled Theban Nile Perche with a soufflé of nightingales eggs,' explained confidently the maître d' as they sat down.

'Sounds great,' said Rex. He looked at Rama. He didn't seem too well and had big rings under his bloodshot eyes. Rama was always an agitated person but since he had received the statue of Hoth he seemed positively wired. Probably up all night talking to it Rex mused. What fascinating conversation they must have.

'What did that mad statue have to say for himself?'

'Quite a lot,' answered Rama. 'Being stuck with Smitheson Smiles and his friendly monks for all those years was enough to get even a statue bored,' he paused and changed the subject to the hotel and the renovations he was carrying out. An extension to the theme park, a new Bedouin styled tent hotel out at one of the oases and strangely a new temple to house the statue. The pasties proved very tasty so Rex didn't interrupt him but let him ramble on while he consumed the whole plate.

'Yea the Bedouin styled oasis hotel should be a great success. It's what fashionable people want these days. A back-to-nature experience in the desert sleeping under the stars. Of course, all the tents will be luxurious and there won't be a Theban mosquito in sight. We stick the kitchens and staff quarters underground near the campsite so we can maintain the view and general rustic ambiance. No need for people to know their food is not cooked over a campfire is there?' Rama talked at one hundred miles per hour. What drugs is he on tonight thought Rex? Total verbal diarrhoea.

'So why a temple for the friendly statue? Mr. Hoth his name?' enquired Rex interrupting the babble.

'Yea Hoth. He says he deserves it ... and he does if everything he says is true,' Rama said. 'He served my ancestors well.' Rama seemed strangely sincere about this. Barking mad was Rex's diagnosis.

'What he served them or they served him?' Rex asked doubtfully. 'What's he proposing? Let me guess? Global domination? Ultimate power? That sort of power crazed thing? He tried it out on me.'

Rama looked a bit nervous about what Rex was saying. His eyes had a haunted look as if he had just signed a pact with the Devil and there was no turning back.

'Kind of ... but things will be better round here you'll see. Nothing to worry about. All good for business,' Rama quickly switched subject. 'Great terrine don't you think. Goes down marvellously with this Karnak Valley chardonnay.'

'Very nice. Wonder where chefy finds all those wild Antares Mega-Buffalo for the terrine? Still, it's great.' Rex kind of knew that wild Antares Mega-Buffalo were an endangered species that had been hunted to the point of extinction but their hooves made great pâté.

'Glad I've finished with that Extreme X Cup nonsense. Too bloody dangerous,' said Rex. 'Lost a foot on Nexus, brave Jonny almost got eaten by an Omega Shark and those mad monks on Hoth will soon be after me for stealing that statue I'm pretty sure.'

'You mean your quitting?' Rama looked surprise or feigned it well.

'Yea, sure. No way am I continuing. It's for crack-pots and adrenaline junkies.' Rex felt good about saying this. He had now publically spelt out his decision and it was final. 'Besides Elmer Diablilo is probably gonna win it. He is just too good.' The fact that Elmer Diablilo was too good had occurred to Rex on several occasions. He never made an error or a false move. There was no point in anybody else being in the competition except to make up the numbers and be cannon fodder so to speak.

'Well it's meant to be dangerous and you don't get billions of dollars for nothing you know.'

The grilled Nile Perche fish arrived and Rama moved swiftly to make his business proposition to Rex.

'Listen, Elmer doesn't have to win you know.'

'How come?' Rex was already tucking into the tasty fish he was getting rather full though and his head was spinning a bit after all the cocktails and bottles of delicious wine they had already drunk. Unfortunately, hot weather always made him drink wine like water.

'Well it is simple, if you do me a little favour, I can fix it so you win.'

'How can you do that? ... And what's the favour?' Rex casually responded. The fish was really good. Optimally grilled he thought. He knew Rama could fix the tournament since he was on the Extreme X Committee and could fix anything. Besides the tournament was probably fixed already but he could not work out how. It just needed re-fixing in his favour.

'So you will win the final and get five billion sweet Andurian dollars ... and all you have to do is pop back in time using that causal violation thingy and pick something up for me. Dead easy, you have done it once already.'

Another silly mission. Rex groaned. 'What do you want this time? ... A scroll? A statue? ... Ain't that enough?'

'Well my granddaddy, another Ramesses of course. Actually Ramesses the tenth to be exact was annoyingly buried with the royal staff or sceptre – called an Hequa Sceptre. It is my inheritance and belongs to me. Selfishly he was annoyed with my dad at the time and buried himself with it. Gave no thought to his future descendants.'

'Oh, I see. Indeed, very selfish of him. Wasn't the tomb found?'

'Yea it was in 1920 local time back on Earth by a buffoon called Sir Thomas Bankes.' Rex knew nothing about Egyptology beyond the marketing hype of the holo-screen, channel 0, in his hotel suite. 'You have got to get there first and recover the sceptre. Nobody knows what happened to it after the tomb was opened so that's the moment in time you have to get back to.'

'Wow that's gotta be almost a 150 year time jump. We have only done smaller jumps up to now. Is it even possible?'

'Yea well I treated the Professor to a free Ionian topless full body massage in the spa...'

'I bet that put a smile on his face,' laughed Rex. Ionian Doppelgangers could turn themselves into whatever or whomever the client wished and they were not bashful.

'Yes, it did a bit. You know academics don't get out much. Anyway, he assured me his device could do the trick if he gets your robot to do the precise time displacement calculations. Apparently, the further back you go in space and time the smaller your error must be.'

'OK, I'll get Dennis working on it.' It sounded easy. A quick trip back to the 1920's on Earth, two more events of Extreme X Cup and he would be wealthy beyond his wildest dreams ... and he had pretty big dreams.

'I knew you couldn't resist,' said Rama. 'I think we should open up a bottle of Vothschild vintage to celebrate. I notice you ran up rather a large tab on Nexus drinking them. The hotel manager there was really annoyed but I took care of it for you ... I always do.'

Chapter Thirty-Four

Dennis had made a really bad landing and stuck the nose of the Eagle into a large sand dune. He claimed that he was slightly disorientated by 150 year time displacement but Rex did not hear his full explanation since his ears were ringing again. Perhaps the Causal Displacement Device still had a slight problem? In any case he found this time travel business rather disconcerting.

Rex and Jonny left the others to dig out the spaceship and set out across the sand. Apparently, it was not too far to the archaeological dig. The Valley of the Kings was only about a mile away. Still it was hot and after a couple of hundred yards up a large dune Jonny was already parched. He wore a baseball cap with a large wave on it from the Omega surf event. Not particularly fitting for the early 1900s but who cared he thought.

'How far is it?' asked Jonny. 'I'm burning to a crisp here.'

'Not far. We should see it soon. Drink some water.' He handed Jonny a flask.

'What are we looking for again?' Rex had not told him the full details except to say there was a fun day of archaeology ahead for all the family, well at least for him and Jonny.

'Rama's granddad's tomb. It's 1920 and some of your English compatriots are digging it up right now as we speak.'

'What does Rama want? Who's digging it up?' Jonny continued the inquisition.

All these questions. Rex's habitual line of vagueness and mystery never worked well with Jonny. Whereas an adult might assume that Rex was either (a) stupid and did not know what he was doing or (b) stupid enough to feign stupidity to avoid telling them, kids like Jonny just thought (c) persistent questioning would wear him down and provide some answers.

'Look. Better if you don't know it all but the guy is called Sir Thomas Bankes, he works for the British Museum and we need to get Rama's granddaddy's staff – it's called the Hequa Sceptre.' That's all he wanted to say but he continued anyway for good measure. 'Apparently Rama was due to inherit it but has been pissed off for over 3000 years that he didn't get his hands on it.'

'Kind of an Indiana Jones mission then?' exclaimed Jonny. It sounded exciting.

'Yea kind of. Good. Got it now? Let's go.'

Jonny had never heard of Thomas Bankes. Howard Carter and Tutankhamen yes but Bankes no. He would later discover there was a good reason for this involving an unforeseen accident with a Hequa Sceptre.

They passed over the top of the dune and below in the valley they saw a small encampment of dusty tents clustered around a rocky outcrop. They ran down the dune towards the dig. Running down sand dunes Jonny discovered was far more pleasurable than staggering up them

Nearby from a large hole in the ground Egyptian locals emerged in their white gowns. It looked like hard, sweaty work climbing up the rickety old ladder lugging heavy straw baskets of stones on their backs. A short distance away a small group of Europeans sat in wicker chairs under a large sunshade.

'Any more tea Harris? These Egyptians do good brew.' Harris, a bearded bespectacled archaeologist nodded. It was probably his $10,000^{th}$ cup of tea at the dig but it helped pass the time and well, teatime was teatime.

Sir Thomas Bankes lounged on his wicker sofa and observed the workers through a pair of Covent Garden opera glasses he had brought with him. They were very effective at watching all the hard, sweaty work from a distance.

'Looks like we should be at the bottom of the shaft pretty soon. Might want Farid to get the Egyptian chappies moving a bit more quickly. Final push and all that.'

Sir Thomas Bankes knew absolutely nothing about Egyptology but an education at Eton and Oxford had provided him with enough Teflon confidence and arrogance to succeed at anything. If he did not succeed and made a complete and total hash of it, he would still be seen as a good sport at his Mayfair club back home. Lesser men in his class had ruled India knowing nothing about administration, stumbled upon important scientific facts knowing absolutely no physics or chemistry or even blundered along with the English economy knowing nothing about economics. Sir Thomas was going to soon make the biggest discovery in Egyptology in the 20th century having only read an undergraduate text book on Egyptology – well he had read the first chapter anyway on the boat out here. The fact that he remains largely unremembered is that knowledge of his discovery would last only about 10 minutes.

Rex wandered up to the makeshift English tearoom. He feared he didn't fully know the protocol of an Englishman's afternoon tea but whatever. A cake-stand of half eaten scones sat on the camping table. Egyptian waiters fussed round serving the tea.

'Hi guys!' He had, he felt, at least attempted to fit in. He knew a thing or two about eccentric academics and had borrowed Professor Mitchell's tweed jacket and necktie and had put on a strange straw hat from Rama's hotel gift shop. He thought he looked the part but the jacket made him sweat a bit. Jonny on the other hand looked a bit out of character sporting an Omega basketball cap and Thebes Waterpark T-shirt.

'Afternoon gentlemen. I am Professor Rogers from the New York Metropolitan Museum Archaeology Department. Is Sir Thomas Bankes here?' If in doubt bluff and bullshit were the best way forward in situations like this. 'I was talking to Howard Carter,' he had found his name in his favourite Egyptology book. Although, he had only read the first chapter as well. All those hawk-headed, dog-headed and other weird gods had become a bit confusing beyond that, '... and he said that I might have something that could help your dig.' He waved a cardboard tube at them temptingly. All of the archaeologists were however fixated by Jonny's trainers. They flickered and swirled in a range of exciting colours with the Mega Hillton and Thebes sphinx head logos appearing and disappearing every few seconds.

'Amazing shoes young man!' exclaimed one particularly doddery old archaeologist, holding his monocle close to his eye. 'How do they do that?'

Rex wanted to say that sub-nanotechnology promotional advertising was now routinely incorporated into a range of useless consumer products these days (which rendered the retail cost to the consumer of zero) but this would probably be lost on his audience.

'Oh, you know kids these days. It's based on a new thing called Nylon, a new type of plastic. We sell them in the Met Museum gift shop in New York.'

He waved the cardboard tube a bit more to distract them. Sir Thomas stood up and held out his hand.

'Good afternoon Professor Rogers. I am Sir Thomas. Looks like we are getting close to something down there. You arrived just in time,' he gestured towards the large hole in the ground. 'What do you have for us?' He did not like that Howard Carter fellow too much. He was a rival and a bit too dedicated. Prepared to spend years in the dirt scrabbling about. Not a technique that would ever lead to anything he thought.

'A previously mis-catalogued scroll from the Met archives. We noticed it gives information on Ramesses X tomb.'

Rex unrolled the scroll on the map table. The archaeologists, all evidently interested, clustered around. It was a copy of part of the scroll Rex had obtained from the British Museum. Rama had had used a nano-replicator. The colours looked old and faded and to the untrained eye without a handy electron microscope it looked like the papyrus original.

'Great Scott! It's about our guy Ramesses!' exclaimed Harris looking carefully at the hieroglyphics through his dusty monocle.

Sir Thomas nodded, apparently knowingly, in agreement. Like Rex, to him hieroglyphics were all a load of mumbo jumbo but as an 'expert' Egyptologist he had to at least pretend to understand them. At least he had had the good sense to bring Harris and Shakeshaft from the Oxford University Archaeology Department as his encyclopaedic backup. Rex couldn't read it either but he had received Rama's vague translation and had it checked by Dennis. He noticed that Rama had been careful to chop the bit off the scroll that mentioned Rama's granddad destroying all his Hittite enemies with a storm of sand, beetles and locusts. Anyway that was Rama's business not his.

'Yes, as far as I can translate it says that the true tomb of the mighty Pharaoh, True Son of Ra, Ramesses X, lies behind the Udjat-Eye,' explained Rex. He tried to sound knowledgeable.

'Very interesting old chap. What does that mean?' another ancient archaeologist, called Shakeshaft, with a large safari hat, chipped in.

'I don't know,' muttered Harris. 'The Udjat-Eye is a neb sign that provides a protective function for the Pharaoh. Usually it is found on powerful protective amulets. Perhaps the American chap knows more?'

They turned and looked at Rex. For all he knew an eye was, well, an eye. At that moment a loud shout came from the pit. The Egyptian workers had found the entrance. One of the workers sprinted eagerly over towards Sir Thomas.

'We have found the bottom Sir Thomas,' he gasped, '... but there is no tomb, Sir!'

'How? What!' Sir Thomas spluttered, spilling his tea in his saucer. He looked both surprised and disappointed. 'That can't be. I mean ...' A true Etonian is not easily deflated though. He grabbed an oil lamp and made for the pit entrance. 'Get everybody out. I want to take a look.' The other two archaeologists rushed behind. Rex and Jonny sauntered slowly after.

No point rushing thought Rex. He had been expecting something like this. Rama had explained that the latest vogue for hiding tombs in his grandfather's period was to make them look like they had not been completed. According to Rama's version of events the local tomb workers of the nearby Deir El-Medina village had become very lazy. Unionisation, restrictive working practices and downright dishonesty had crept into the workforce which had pissed-off successive Pharaohs. No sooner did they finish a tomb for a dignitary than they would tip off their cousins from the neighbouring valley who would then systematically loot it. Apparently, tomb robbery had become big business for organised crime.

They all climbed down the wooden ladder into the pit. At the bottom, amid the flickering torches, the rough hewn tunnel opened into a downward sloping passage. Worn Egyptian frescos covered the walls. A real Egyptian tomb thought Jonny, and it smelt real bad. He held his nose, the stale air smelt of bad damp. Probably flood damage since the plastered bottom of the nearest frescos had fallen away. They descended the passage for about twenty yards then came to a partially hewn rock face blocking the passage.

'Bugger! Bugger!' shouted Sir Thomas repeatedly kicking the wall, visibly annoyed.

'Looks like he never finished it,' said Harris.

'Damn shame what! Maybe they ran out of money?' followed Shakeshaft fingering the sold but crumbly stone.

They were all visibly extremely disappointed. Jonny was too. He had been dying to see a real Egyptian sarcophagus or even better a real Egyptian mummy.

Rex shone the lamp against the nearby walls and looked around. Rama had told him to locate a large, unmistakable eye. Almost immediately he located a large eye, painted bright blue, at shoulder height beside him.

'Gentlemen,' he paused momentarily to make his announcement more grandiose. 'Here is the Udjat-Eye! Remember the scroll?'

'Well spotted old chap.'

'But what does it signify?' asked Harris.

Rex took up a shovel one of the workers had left nearby. He swung it against the eye.

'Steady old boy. That's a priceless fresco,' Harris looked worried.

Rex ignored him and swung again even harder. The plaster cracked and fell away. Behind there was darkness, a void.

'Another passage!' exclaimed an excited Sir Thomas. Treasures, discovery, fame and fortune were more interesting than the preservation of more tedious wall paintings. He picked up another shovel and helped enlarge the opening.

Behind the thin plaster wall, another steeper passage led away into the hillside. It smelt different. It was dry and musty inside. The brightly coloured frescos had never seen sunlight and were perfectly preserved.

Large figures of Osiris, his son Horus, Thoth and Anubis lead down the passageway. These gave way to a gleaming Pharaoh sailing on a sunboat and Egyptians working in fields.

There was a large image of the Pharaoh riding a golden chariot pulled by lions slaying a horde of enemies. It was all preserved in breathtaking Technicolor. The English Egyptologists were dumbfounded. Jonny thought it was very cool. Rex, unimpressed, just thought that, apart from the battle scene, it looked just like the casino in the Thebes hotel.

'Amazing. Completely amazing,' said Sir Thomas completely flabbergasted. He knew he was on to something truly big. He was going to be the most celebrated Egyptologist ever. Bigger than his hero the Italian Titan of Padua, Belzoni!

'Could be the biggest find of the century!' enthused Shakeshaft.

Sir Thomas ran down the corridor. One thought was in his head. Was the tomb and its treasure intact? The other archaeologists enthusiastically skipped after him as fast as their doddery old legs would allow.

'Hang on boys. Be careful,' cried Rex after them. He only wanted one thing – the Pharaoh's sceptre. In return Rama had promised him a win in the Extreme X Cup ... five billion Andurian dollars prize money. Jonny wanted to run after the excited Egyptogists but Rex held him by the shoulder. In the back of his mind he knew that if Rama's ancestors were half as cunning as Rama, they might have a few tricks up their sleeve. Rama had given him precise instructions how to disarm the sceptre when they found it.

At the bottom of the passage was a large funery chamber supported by six pillars. Each represented a familiar god and the sixth was obviously the Pharaoh. In the middle was a rectangular pit. It was full almost to the brim of blackish, oily looking water. It didn't smell too good. The archaeologists were nowhere to be seen. They had disappeared down a corridor at the other side of the room. Rex could hear their excited voices and see lamplight flickering against the walls.

'We found it!!' Sir Thomas shouted. 'Yahoo! We found it!'

'Incredible. Look at that!' said another voice. It sounded like a bunch of school children in a sweet shop.

Rex and Jonny followed down the second passage. What he saw amazed even a major cynic like him. He might have seen a few big cheques, suitcases of money or large mounds of gambling chips but here was real, tangible wealth. The small burial chamber was filled from ceiling to floor with the most amazing things. Two life-size wooden statues painted black and gold stood by the door. Beyond them a large statue of Anubis atop a wooden coffer lay to one side next to a couple of golden couches decorated with lion headed goddesses. Wheels of a dismantled golden, gilded chariot lay to the other side leaning against a huge model sunboat or barge complete with a model crew, which looked remarkably like a scaled down version of Rama's full scale replica. Everywhere there lay boxes and coffers and urns inlaid with scintillating, coloured precious stones. Rex could see that some boxes lay open and contained gold coins, exquisite jewellery and other artefacts such as lamps, weapons and armour. These Pharaohs certainly knew how to live, even in death, Rex thought.

In the centre was a massive, reddish sarcophagus. On top lay an ornate jewelled golden sceptre. The top was bent in the form of a large hook. It was the Hequa-Sceptre Rex was searching for.

'Hey look at this ...' Sir Thomas saw it first. He felt drawn to it. He had never seen anything quite so beautiful. Despite the dust the jewels still shone like miniature red, blue and green stars.

'Please don't touch that!' Rex shouted anxiously.

'Why ever not?' Sir Thomas Bankes, soon to be renowned archaeologist picked it up. No coarse Yank was going to tell a great Egyptologist like him what he could do. The sceptre throbbed and hummed in his hand. It seemed to radiate power.

It made him feel strong and regal. 'Behold the great Pharaoh Bankes,' he joked.

Rex who had started discretely pilling one or two interesting trinkets into his bag, stopped and grabbed Jonny's hand. He ran for the exit. He had a sudden premonition something bad was going to happen. Why would Rama tell him it needed disarming if it were perfectly safe?

'The buttons! Press the Ankh three times,' he cried to Sir Thomas who was not listening. He was looking at the sceptre in amazement. From the sceptre sand gusted in a growing, swirling cloud. Rex and Jonny ran back up the ramp into the tunnel. The chamber was filling with the swirling cloud. Quickly, in a whistling vortex it enveloped the three archaeologists. Harris and Shakeshaft held their hands over their eyes and mouths and stumbled for the exit. The sand howled and twisted around them tearing at their flesh. Faster Rex and Jonny ran down the passage the dust clouds billowing behind them. They reached the previous ante-chamber and Rex pushed Jonny and himself into the oily water pit.

'I know it stinks but hold your breath for as long as possible.'

The water stunk but neither of them complained. There was no alternative. The water enveloped them and they could not touch the bottom. The sand clouds screamed madly over their heads. In the water it was silent and black. Rex held Jonny gently beneath the surface. Both of them tried not to panic. Rex counted slowly for as long as possible. He ran out of breath before Jonny and broke the surface. It was complete blackness. Not a sound. He climbed out of the stinking pit and dragged out Jonny. Rex fumbled in his backpack for his flashlight. Looking around the sand had disappeared as quickly as it had arrived.

'Looks all clear,' he whispered to Jonny.

'There is no sign of Bankes and the others,' said Jonny.

They walked downstairs towards the tomb. Rex tripped over something heavy. It was the sceptre lying innocuously in the passageway. Next to it was a suspicious pile of white dust.

'That's Sir Thomas I think?' Rex was shocked. What was this thing? He did not usually start to believe in superstition or magic except at extreme moments like this.

Jonny was shocked too. 'Poor Sir Thomas. That thing's really dangerous. Be careful.'

'Don't worry. I kind of know that now.'

Rex shone the flashlight over to the corner. Two more piles of dust lay on the floor. A broken monocle lay on one of the piles. Presumably Harris and Shakeshaft. The sceptre, now lying innocently on the floor, was obviously pretty meticulous in dishing out the punishment. Without touching it he located a few symbols on the shaft of the sceptre. Some form of buttons or hand control he thought. He felt comforted that it was a machine not magic. Probably some form of nano-tech defence mechanism concealed in the ancient artefact. Obviously not domestic Egyptian technology. Where had the Pharaoh's got this from? He pressed the button labelled with the Ankh symbol tree times. He picked it up and anxiously awaited. Nothing happened. Maybe, hopefully he had disarmed it. He placed the sceptre carefully in his backpack and after helping himself to a few more choice trinkets they made their way out of the tomb into the blinding sunlight. Outside the camp was deserted, a couple of tents had been blown down and the Egyptian workers were gone. Whether they had simply run away or been obliterated it was hard to tell amidst all the sand. As Rama had requested, Rex threw a small thermite grenade into the hidden entranceway to seal the tomb. There was a loud explosion and Ramesses X tomb was sealed forever. Still dripping with the stinking oily water, they made their way back to the spaceship.

Chapter Thirty-Five

Usually in an extreme sports competition some form of free climbing event would be included. However, visually for the billions of spectators, watching climbers in action was as boring as watching paint dry or almost as dull as a test match in Callistan cricket, celebrated as the most monotonous sport in the Galaxy, where the innings could often exceed the lifetime of the players. The media types decided climbing was just too slow moving and lacking in action. Sometimes someone would fall off a cliff or pinnacle but if you blinked or popped out to make a cup of tea you missed it. Instead, the Extreme X Cup Organising Committee usually held an extreme ski or some form of risky ski-mountaineering event in the Summit system. Unfortunately, to Blofield Blatus's dismay the weather on the two ski resort planets in the Summit system had been abominable for months. A 'white out' did not make for good holo-vision. So instead, one day sitting in his whirl-bath and talking to his beloved but carefully chained up Tyrossian Pterodactyl, he concocted a totally new event. One that he was very proud of and was sure would provide much entertainment to his viewers and sponsors – jet-pack canyoning. Rex would later remark that only a complete imbecile or lover of extremely dangerous birds of prey could come up with such a totally stupid event and that saying something since he thought most of the events were totally insane. For him it was the final proof that the whole tournament was the product of a deranged mind.

Rama however thought it was a truly inspired event and worthy of a genius and voted for it at the impromptu committee meeting. It would provide a perfect way for him to get rid of Rex as the statue now desired. Rex should have realised that a woman spurned is dangerous enough but spurning the statue of Hoth was fatal. Even minor deities do not like rejection. Now actually Rama felt somewhat sad because he really quite liked Rex but he had to obey Him. With Hoth it was easier to go with the flow rather than object and be chastised.

Chapter Thirty-Six

'These people are crazy! Jet-pack canyoning? What the hell is that?' exclaimed Chiva the Iguanadon downing another Argossian beer.

'Blatus had the idea in his bath apparently,' stirred Rex. Largus the Octi-man came back from the bar with another round of drinks. He did not need a tray. Tentacles and suckers did the trick.

'I was looking forward to the ski event. I had been training especially for it,' moaned Chiva. He was agitated and his dorsal fin had chewed up the faux leather sofa.

'And how do I get a jet-pack to fit?' questioned Vodos the remaining Blue-Goo. He had an interesting way of drinking beer mused Rex. Just kind of sat on the glass and absorbed the drink. Perhaps osmosis or something?

'Well the worst thing apparently is those Tyrossian Pterodactyls. The canyon is infested with them,' chipped in the Callistan Mudskipper. Strange creature, Rex didn't know his name. His big bulging eyes had the convenient capability of being able to turn full 360 degrees during a conversation as he checked out the girls at the bar. It was a very disconcerting habit. Rex could not imagine what girls would be interested in a slimy mudskipper. Maybe he had good conversation?

Normally Rex tried to avoid pre-event drinks. He always wondered whether he psyched out the other competitors more that they psyched him out. He had to admit though they were occasionally quite interesting especially when they all had something to moan about. Rex always secretly hoped he could catalyse some kind of revolution but here everybody was too focused on winning the 5 billion dollars. There were six of them left in the competition. Elmer Diablilo and the Mega-Troll competitor had perhaps wisely not bothered to turn up.

'Yes Blatus has a pet Pterodactyl. If one or two of us get eaten it makes for good ratings,' cynically added Largus handing out several beers simultaneously. The conversation meandered into speculation as to whether a heavy Spinozan Iguanadon wearing a jet-pack on full blast could outrun a gaggle of Pterodactyls. They wondered, laughing, what would be the fastest reptile. Rex drank up quickly, an early night was needed before the event.

He retired to his hotel room feeling unusually rather optimistic. He was sure he could fly faster than an Iguanadon and was more aerodynamic than Blue-Goo. More importantly he had forgotten to tell the others that as a kid eight-a-side jet-pack airball had been one of his favourite hobbies. His university scholarship had been as an airball striker.

Chapter Thirty-Seven

Tyrossa's World was a hot, fertile, savage planet. It was one of those places where if you lingered to admire the view or stopped to tie your shoe lace you would probably be eaten by some giant lizard who would probably be eaten by an even bigger lizard whilst it was lunching on you. Lizards and snakes of assorted sizes were everywhere and even the plants had a voracious appetite. Evolutionary complexity had lead to some spectacular life-forms and the planet was a favourite amongst galactic big game hunters. Despite numerous warnings not to leave the hotel enclosure several spectators had already gone missing in the surrounding jungle and were presumed eaten.

'Well Ant. Today is another exciting day in the Extreme X Cup. Due to adverse weather conditions on Summit we welcome you to Round Four on Tyrossa's World for a day of extreme jet-pack canyoning.'

'Yes Dec. Tyrossa's World is well known for its spectacular and friendly wildlife and today is no exception. Here we have a fine example – a Tyrossian Pterodactyl.'

The camera showed a huge, massively beaked reptile. Its leathery wings folded behind it as it sat on a podium. Probably drugged or had a force screen round it thought Rex since otherwise it would have most likely ripped one of Anton Werhofer's arms off. Now that would have made for good programming.

'Yea Ant, he looks rather cute. They will be keeping our six final competitors' company on the course today,' the presenter smiled, displaying his perfect dentures. The Pterodactyl's teeth looked uglier and more infrequently brushed but much more efficient. 'Remember there are eight gates that the competitors must clear today. Each missed gate costs the competitor a three minute penalty.'

'Fastest two go through to the final and the chance to win five billion cool Andurian crypto-dollars.' The commentary continued and showed a birds-eye view of the course. A windy 50 mile stretch of the Zoroaster canyon. Mostly a few hundred yards wide and about a mile deep but narrowing to below 50 yards in places. A flying camera followed the course so the spectators would have a preview of the dangers that awaited. Yellow flashing gates were placed along the course. Each gate was three to four yards wide and would flash green if a competitor passed through and changed red on a miss. Tyrossian Pterodactyls were mysteriously absent from the walk through.

Chapter Thirty-Eight

Curiously Elmer Diablilo was first in the draw again. Rex didn't even bother to watch. It was kind of predictable. A cheer went up from the holo-screen as Elmer perfectly navigated each gate. He scored a supposedly fast time.

Vodos the Blue-Goo was second. He had difficulty controlling his jet-pack and navigating the canyon. A couple of Pterodactyls flapped curiously by him and decided Blue-Goo was probably not too appetising. The commentators speculated that they preferred flesh and blood and were probably waiting for a nice tasty limb. He seemed a bit disorientated, missed three gates and was visibly disappointed on the screen.

It was Rex's turn next. From the top of the canyon, it did not look too inviting. Ferns and vines cascaded down the canyon walls. He could hear the squawk and cries of strange wildlife in the misty forest far below. He checked his jet-pack and it started smoothly with a low whine of the twin turbojets. The organisers were obviously cutting costs again since the jet-pack was old fashioned and even the paint was peeling off. Rex hadn't seen one like this for years and he hoped it was up to the job; his life depended on it. The starting droid gave him the green light and Rex hurtled downwards into the canyon. He made for the first gate a few hundred metres beneath him. A few seconds later he passed through it.

'Well done. First gate,' it chimed cheerfully and promptly turned green. The gate seemed very satisfied he had done another good job for the pleasure of another competitor.

The next gate was a couple of minutes away near the canyon floor. Rex followed the trail of the river as it cascaded along the bottom of the canyon. Down here it seemed almost primordial as large ferns bordered the rocky, boulder strewn river. As he flew past he could hear frightening bestial noises from the undergrowth. Huge, indescribable bugs hit his visor as he flew low across the water. The next gate was ahead at the edge of a large spectacular waterfall. It congratulated him as he flew through it and down the waterfall towards gate three. Past gate three at the end of a large lake the canyon narrowed into a further torrent. Towards the narrowing he could see two Pterodactyls converging with his trajectory. He dipped lower towards the water. He reckoned he would just get to the narrowing before them but just in case he reached for his sonic security knife. The security knife was the only allowed 'weapon' in the event rules. It was really only to be used in the event of a crash landing in the jungle or to cut loose the jet-pack in case of a burn-out. Still Rex reasoned it probably would prove some defence against hungry Pterodactyls. He reached the narrowing before the Pterodactyls and sped between the cliffs. The Pterodactyls were about twenty yards away from him and unfortunately, since they had only had a light breakfast, they decided to follow him down the narrow canyon. The winding walls made it difficult to fly fast. Rex did his best navigating between the outcrops and overhangs. A couple of camera droids struggled to keep up and bounced and scrapped against the rocks. He released the jet-pack throttle on any straight section and applied reverse thrust on some of the tight bends. He looked round. The Pterodactyls were obviously used to these conditions and were closing on him. Their primordial shrieks filled his ears. They knew where their next meal was coming from. 10, 5, 3, 2 yards away from Rex, their snapping beaks came closer. He could feel the blast from their leathery wings.

At the last second Rex hit full reverse thrust. It threw him into the chest of a surprised Pterodactyl, which let out a large annoyed squawk. Rex plunged the sonic knife into its neck. The vibrating blade cut effortlessly through the tough hide of the beast. Dark red blood sprayed over Rex who, suffering from a loss of airspeed, plunged towards the torrent below. Rex quickly fumbled for the forward thrust button and accelerated just before getting his feet wet. The second Pterodactyl was high above him and looked like it had temporarily given up chase. Rex breathed a sigh of relief and headed towards the next couple of gates.

The canyon opened out once more into what seemed a huge amphitheatre surrounded by sheer cliffs. There was one gate left above the jungle at the bottom of the canyon. Rex steered towards it, rubbing blood from his visor and looked around. Behind him, flying from the cliffs were at least a dozen Pterodactyls speeding towards him. They were still some distance away. Maybe he could make the last gate and get out of the canyon before they caught up with him. He pushed maximum thrust and hurtled towards the last gate.

'Well done. Congratulations you have made the last gate!' the gate happily announced.

The Pterodactyls were now converging on him from all sides. He pushed the thrust button even harder and headed for the cliffs, skimming the forest canopy below, trying to fly under the leathery birds. At the last minute he pitched himself into a steep climb. Steeper and steeper to climb out of the canyon. Suddenly something went wrong. The guidance grip seemed unresponsive. There was no control. The rocky cliff face loomed before him. Rex tried to reduce his speed but reverse thrust was jammed. A total jet-pack malfunction.

'Oh, no ... not again!' he thought as his helmet impacted against the cliff face.

Chapter Thirty-Nine

Was this heaven thought Rex briefly? He thought the impact against the cliff face would have felt more painful at some point but he could not recollect it. Still the chair was comfortable so maybe heaven was a comfy chair. Although he didn't really believe in Heaven he thought, despite his limited imagination, that a comfy chair would have been a bit of a cosmic underachievement.

'Hello Mr. Rogers.'

Rex recognised the pedantic law-abiding tone. He had heard it somewhere before. He opened one eye and looked around. It was the two Chrono Police officers or whatever they called themselves. The room was white or rather a subtle shade of light grey with no doors or windows visible. No immediate chance of escape this time. Much to his displeasure they had him and would probably subject him to 'you've been a bad boy Mr. Rogers' lecture. Maybe to make it more interesting they would adopt a good-cop, bad-cop routine. Still, at least they had saved him from a potentially fatal series of multiple fractures.

'You are probably feeling a bit disorientated'

Rex grunted. 'Yea where am I? What happened? Who are you?' he decided to get his questions in before they did.

'I am Chrono Constable Alurari. We saved you from a fatal accident or rather a fatal assassination.'

'Assassination?' That was news to Rex. Who wanted to try to kill him apart from a very long list of people he already knew about?

'Mr. Ramesses. A particularly unstable character who has caused us much concern recently.'

'Rama? But why would he want to do that? We had a deal.'

'Ah ... your misuse of an unlicensed Causal Flux Generator has caused many things to change in an undesirable way,' continued Constable Alurari.

'What do you mean?' He had realised with his little betting experience on Nexus that reality was a bit more complicated than it first appeared.

'Well since they fixed the poker game you have embarked on a series of events that have disrupted the future and the past to the great discomfort of many people.'

'They fixed the poker match! I knew it! I knew it! Bastards!' This rather than the apparent discomfort of the Galaxy's inhabitants was Rex's major concern. It was a revelation to Rex but deep inside his ego told him that he was not that bad at poker. Rama had encouraged him to play the Big Table poker game. He had lent him the money since Rex could not afford the stakes. They were all a bunch of lousy corrupt billionaire cockroaches – Rama, Lazard Bond, Felix Rohtyn the advertising and media mogul, General Eduargo military man and suspected black-market arms dealer and Commissioner Dreyfus the most corruptible civil servant in charge of mining and mineral extraction rights. He was really, really annoyed he had been setup.

'The so-called Statue of Hoth has been known to appear in various places in our space-time continuum and always causes trouble.'

'What exactly is it?' enquired Rex. He was more interested imagining what he would do with Lazard Bond and the others with his boot if they really were the size of cockroaches.

'It is the manifestation of an egotistic pan-dimensional entity representing a pantheon of minor deities.' Rex did not understand but to imagine something more egotistical than himself was difficult as he was frequently reminded by most of his family.

'Sounds like bad news.'

'It is. By retrieving the statue from Hoth, where it was only causing minor suffering, you have managed to extend its control and suffering amongst over a trillion of the Galaxy's sentient beings.' The second Chrono Constable spoke. He was visibly a bit more annoyed by Rex's role in events.

For an instant Rex started to feel guilty. But surely, they were just bluffing. The old good cop, bad cop routine?

'Well, Hoth didn't seem too bad. I mean he is just going to keep Rama company on Thebes. He might brainwash a few fat tourists but that's about it.' He tried a weak laugh to lighten the atmosphere.

'Through the suggestive hypnosis of over a trillion people at the live broadcast of the final of the Extreme X Cup, Hoth using Mr Ramesses will enslave a large fraction of the Outer Spiral Rim in your Galaxy. We can't let this happen.'

'What can I do about it? I mean I am just an unfortunate pawn in a game by the big boys.' Rex adopted an 'I am completely useless fool caught up in all this' strategy.

'Mr. Rogers. I don't think you realise the seriousness of the offense you have committed. Misuse of a Causal Violation Device is punishable by up to 1000 years imprisonment under regulation 53.2 of the Pan Galactic Council.'

'Come on guys you're bluffing?' What was the Pan Galactic Council anyway? He had never heard of it. 'How can I be accused of a crime if I didn't know it was a crime?' He suspected it actually might not matter since last time he was given a speeding ticket he did not realise it was a planetary speed restricted zone (or pretended he didn't since Dennis did try and warn him).

'Unfortunately, ignorance is not a valid defence. We tried to warn you on Earth but you resisted arrest.' Rex wished he had more chocolate in his pocket but he didn't.

'OK so you want to cut a deal? Waive my sentence for my crimes against causality for info or something. I don't mind squealing.' He didn't know what he could squeal about since they knew much more than him anyway.

'Yes, that's the general idea Mr. Rogers.'

'At the next Extreme X event Mr. Ramesses will be there. You cannot let him address the public with the sceptre. The Hequa Sceptre was engineered to provide a conduit for the Statue of Hoth. In addition, the statue must be seized and removed to a safe location. It cannot be destroyed as such at this time.'

In theory it sounded straight forward thought Rex. But he did not really believe these guys. I mean did Rama really intend to kill him? And if the Galaxy was destined to enjoy a future of fine Egyptian dining and Rama's *prêt-a-porter* surely that was not so bad?

Chapter Forty

'Oh no!! He is gonna hit the cliff!' Panos quickly covered her eyes with her tail.
'Or the Pterodactyls are going to get him!' said Jonny anxiously.
'My goodness gracious! How very exciting!' Professor Mitchell dropped the entire bowl of nachos covered with his favourite spicy Ligronian cheese, that Dennis had lovingly prepared, on the floor.
They had seen the entire event on the giant holo-screen in the ship's lounge. They had prepared for it well ... nachos with Argossian beer for the Professor and synthetic Vegan fruit smoothies for Jonny and sat glued to the edge of their sofas. Although the jet-pack canyoning event had started rather boringly the appearance of the Tyrossian Pterodactyls had soon livened things up. Panos, who unlike the others had lost her appetite, was very proud of Rex's jet-pack ability. She knew he played airball years ago but didn't know he was this good. Jonny and Professor Mitchell were virtually speechless as Rex had navigated down the winding canyon and fought the two Pterodactyls. Now they could see Rex, covered in dark Pterodactyl's blood moving at full throttle towards the finish. An evidently hungry gaggle of Pterodactyls were rapidly converging on him. After passing the last gate Rex pitched the jet-pack into a very steep climb before the high cliff. It was going to be a very close shave. He had so much speed how was he not going to hit the cliff?
'He is never going to make it!' cried Panos. She looked very worried and Jonny put his arm round her. He had never seen her so emotional. She obviously cared about Rex a lot he thought.

The Professor unsuccessfully tried to recover the nachos whilst keeping his eyes fixed on the screen. He dropped the bowl again, so Dennis moved in to pick them up obscuring the screen to everyone's annoyance.

'On the available data I compute a less than 1 in 10 chance of Sir Rex not impacting the cliff at this velocity,' remarked Dennis monotonously.

'Shut up! You and your stupid probabilities! Get outta the way!' Panos threw her empty beer can at Dennis.

To Dennis the impact of Rex against the cliff was virtually inevitable based on the known laws of physics. He had deliberately wrongly rounded up the statistics to give everyone at least a false sense of hope in an attempt to cheer everyone up. Sentient organic beings generally liked the notion of hope he had long since discovered.

But somehow something strange then happened. One moment Rex was flying directly at the cliff and the next moment he was travelling vertically upwards parallel to the cliff face. Dennis and all his circuits wondered how such an instantaneous change of momentum could be achieved. Something fishy had happened ... an un-computable physical paradox. But somehow the others, as with over one trillion other live spectators, had completely bought it and thought nothing was wrong. 'Lucky Rex Rogers lives again!' the presenters cried. The Pterodactyls were not so lucky and some of them in their over-whelming enthusiasm for live flesh, ploughed into the solid immutable cliff face.

'Amazing skill! Rex your great!' Panos jumped up from her chair in glee knocking the Professor's nachos over the floor again. 'Told you he could do it!' She poked her long Tremote tongue out at Dennis.

Dennis shuffled off, the phone had just started ringing. He was glad his master Rex was still alive although disappointed the laws of physics had been violated. He replayed the holo-image in his deepest circuits in slow motion and tried to find a reason or an explanation of how Rex had undermined the basic laws of classical mechanics. But there it was, one frame Rex was travelling towards the cliff and the next he wasn't. It was like a massive unseen instantaneous force had changed Rex's momentum without reducing Rex to strawberry jam. He picked up the phone. Some apparently important guy wanting to give Rex a job with his airball team. He politely took the message but the phone rang again and it continued like that for several hours. Rex Rogers had become an instantaneous celebrity – at least amongst the dedicated fans of the Extreme X Cup. Elmer Diablilo was boring apparently but in the words of one frantic caller, 'Rex Rogers was a mega cool dude.' In the end Dennis gave up and switched on the answer phone. His master would be home soon with his expansive ego even more expansive than usual.

Chapter Forty-One

It was two weeks to the final and Blofield Blatus was enjoying a well-deserved vacation on Thebes. The fact that the cost of the luxurious hotel suite did not impact his personal bank balance made the holiday even more enjoyable. The competition was a success again for another year and the jet-pack canyoning event, as he predicted, had proved a big hit with the viewers and fans.

He strolled along the immaculately weeded path towards Rama's villa set amidst the palm grove. Gorgeous semi-tropical flowers bordered the path. He was looking forward to his lunch. Rama had a great personal chef and Blatus had tried to poach him several times to work on his star-yacht. He generally found Rama relatively harmless and suitably deferential. Mega Hillton's sponsorship was crucial to the success of the Extreme X Cup each year. Also, he thoroughly enjoyed the annual two week expenses paid vacation on Thebes as Rama's special guest. He rang the ostentatious doorbell shaped like a sphinx's head.

'Good afternoon Mr. Blatus.' Rama's ancient butler answered the door.

'Afternoon James,' Blatus replied.

'Mr. Ramesses apologises but he is just finishing a call. Please come in. Would you like an aperitif while you are waiting?'

James showed him through the extravagant, double height lounge filled with Egyptian sculptures and curiosities mingled with expensive modern art and onto the terrace overlooking the pool. The pool was again shaped like a sphinx's head (a common theme thought Blatus) and from it you could see down the hill towards the Karnak Temple complex that was actually one of the largest casinos in the Outer Spiral Rim.

A few minutes later Rama appeared in all his Egyptian regalia holding a bejewelled sceptre. Now although Rama could pretend to like all his lazy guests here was someone who really made the top of his hate list. In his view Blofield Blatus was a dishonourable, short, bald, fat man who knew no bounds for corruption, bribery and kick-backs. Rama was fed up with trying to ingratiate himself with the loathsome toad for all these years. He was eager to try out his ancestors' sceptre on Blatus. As Deputy Chairman of the Organising Committee, he would first restore credibility to the Extreme X Cup before restoring honest Pharonic rule to the Galactic Rim.

'Afternoon Blatus. Hope you are enjoying yourself.'

'Yes, having a great time as always. The Deputy Chairman knows how to show the Chairman a good time,' Blatus laughed.

'What are you drinking Blatus?' asked Rama severely.

'A Theban Kir. James just made it. Very tasty.' A red-looking liquid bubbled ferociously in a stylish long glass.

'Good nothing to strong. I don't want your sensation to be too dulled,' Rama grinned manically.

To Blatus's surprise Rama lifted up the sceptre, concentrated hard and muttered a few incantations. The Hequa Sceptre understood his new master. It had waited a long, dark time buried in the tomb. A cloud of sand swirled forth from the sceptre and immediately engulfed the amazed Blatus who didn't even have enough time to put down his cocktail glass. Blatus's screams were muffled by the swirling cloud of sand particles as they stripped the flesh from his body. Within a couple of seconds his body was sand blasted to its bare bones and Blatus's fat bald head was reduced to a parched, leering skull, mouth open wide either in pain or astonishment. There was a short cracking sound and the skeleton crumbled into a pile of dust. The sand particles, knowing they had done a good job, swirled back into tiny orifices hidden in the sceptre very pleased with themselves. It was a long time since they had seen this much action and their last master had preferred the flesh-eating scarab function. Most effective thought Rama as he prodded with his toe the pile of dust that was once the odious Blofield Blatus. He picked up the phone and called the maid to sweep up. Now he was de facto head of the Extreme X Cup Committee. There would be no more whingeing and moaning about his hotel Egyptian cotton sheets being the wrong weight, the room service being slow and his restaurant not being worth a Michelin star. He smiled to himself and tucked into the delicious prawn cocktail and vine salad his chef had so carefully prepared.

Chapter Forty-Two

Rex had decided he needed to check things out for himself. Surely the future could not be so bad, could it? He never liked to trust a policeman. He spent most of his life avoiding them after all. They had arrived in orbit around Thebes two years in the future and things already looked bleak. They were all gathered round the holo-vision in the ship's lounge.

'Good to see that the downward spiral of entertainment quality continues into the future,' muttered Rex.

'Wait this one looks interesting,' said Jonny as he zapped through the channels. A programme called the 'Hoth Factor' appeared to be in progress. A reality talent show, where young spotty teenagers appeared to be singing hymns to the god Hoth. Every channel had become dedicated to religious content. Although only one god was featured: the 'glorious and just' Hoth. Religious talk shows debated how Hoth could solve your personal problems ranging from alcoholism, marriage breakdowns and teenage pregnancies. Sermons to followers of Hoth were being preached on every other channel and everywhere you looked were images of a shining, smiling Rama looking far too wise and benevolent.

'Okay, from here things are starting to look bad,' announced Rex. 'We need to check this out more closely.'

He wondered if he had seen enough but before throwing away the final of the Extreme X Cup and five billion Andurian dollars he wanted to be absolutely convinced.

'Dennis take us in for a landing.'

As they approached Thebes, Dennis reappeared. 'We are being hailed from the surface Sir Rex.' Through the viewport Rex could see assorted Federal Naval vessels including a couple of Sentinel Class Battlecruisers.

'This is Thebes control. Please give your identity. Only pilgrim vessels are currently allowed to land.' The flight controller sounded terribly bored.

Rex improvised. 'This is pilgrim vessel Eagle from Vega. We request permission to land.'

There was a brief silence. The controller wondered whether his job really had any justification since every vessel, these days, was a pilgrim vessel. His only power was to make them wait a few anxious minutes before replying

'Eagle you are cleared to land. The festivities in honour of Hoth are shortly due to commence. Please proceed directly to Karnak spaceport.'

They touched down at the spaceport. It was very busy and numerous ships and liner shuttles were already there. The shuttles disgorged lines of robe clad visitors who were shepherded by large, hawk-headed security guards towards a newly built stadium.

'Those guys look pretty serious,' observed Rex.

'Those are the robots I was telling you about,' chipped in Jonny.

'Security droids manufactured by Syrus Droid Foundries,' added Dennis.

'So let's go and see what's happening in there. I'll go with Panos and you guys stay here and whatever you do don't leave the ship.' Rex tried to show a bit of leadership.

'What do we wear?' asked Panos. 'All those pilgrim guys have robes.'

They had no proper robes but Dennis, showing surprising originality for a robot, suggested the Egyptian tourist robes they had worn to a particularly dull fancy dress party on Thebes a few months ago. Panos grabbed a hand-blaster and concealed it beneath her robe.

They fell in line with the other pilgrims and made their way towards the huge ten story high stadium. It was thought Rex kind of reminiscent of the coliseum on Maximus he had once been to. Ringed by artificial sand stone arches supported by pillars of jackal-headed gods the stadium dominated the surrounding countryside.

'Looks like your friend Rama's ego has gone overboard,' joked Panos looking at the flags emblazoned with Rama's head that fluttered from the top of the stadium.

'Yes well he always loved construction projects but previously they were financially constrained even though his ego wasn't.'

Inside it was packed with a couple of hundred thousand so-called pilgrims talking in low, hushed voices. Amidst the crowds nobody noticed them and they took a seat and waited for the gig to start. Rex wondered who was headlining but he could probably guess.

A few minutes later and a silence fell across the crowd. An anticipation of a great moment seemed to hold the spectators.

'His Supreme Galactic Pharaoh and Sacred Son of Hoth, Ramesses I of the New Egyptian Empire welcomes you,' boomed speakers concealed around the stadium.

At the far end Rama appeared, resplendent in his crown, jewelled robes and holding the sceptre Rex had recently foolishly recovered. He stood at a pulpit and a giant viewscreen above the stadium broadcast Rama's face. He looked serious, not smiling and there was a mad sheen that twinkled in his eyes.

What happened next Rex found distinctly unsettling and made holo-vision evangelists seem like rank amateurs. Rama immediately started to lead the devoted masses in some form of prayer. His guttural voice cried across the stadium. The acoustics were amazing thought Rex but what language was this? He understood several but this sounded like someone trying to read the menu in one of Rama's hotels. Nobody could ever understand how to pronounce the pretentious, funny sounding main courses and only could read the translation beneath 'roasted chicken served with couscous and red pepper sauce.' This was obviously a bit more meaningful but less tasty than roasted chicken. A vision of the statue of Hoth was relayed onto the holo-screen above the coliseum. Obviously, they did not need to move the statue from its place of security, just relay its image to the worshippers. Or maybe, as the Chrono Police had predicted, the relay was the Hequa Sceptre held by Rama? In any case the effect of ancient Egyptian prayer and the image of Hoth started to have an immediate effect on Rex. He looked around him. The crowd rocked and swayed, transfixed, chanting in low voices. Rex's brain felt like a veil was gradually falling over his consciousness. Some form of mass hypnosis maybe? A giant, unseen hand seemed to be tugging at him, drawing him under. He recalled he had been to a strange hippy transcendental meditation camp in the forest years before and had experienced a similar, although weaker sensation before, slightly disappointed, asking for his money back. A familiar voice entered his head.

'Welcome Rex. You have come back to join us. Now I am strong. You cannot resist me ...' It was the Statue of Hoth.

Panos shook him by the shoulder. Rex snapped out of it.

'Let's get out of this nut house,' Panos anxiously whispered.

'Sure thing. Couldn't agree more. Let's go.'

Rex pushed his way out towards the nearest exit. At the bottom of the stairs another familiar face greeted them. An unsmiling Amelia looking rather more unwelcoming than usual and three large hawk-headed security droids. They wielded assorted heavy weapons that Rex thought could probably turn him into toast in an instant.

'Hands up guys,' said Amelia. She did not seem to be messing around. Rex decided that temporary surrender rather than being toast was presently the best option. He and Panos put their hands up.

'Hi Amelia. Nice show Rama's got here bet it's a sell out.'

'Yes. The grateful pilgrims come here every day from across the Galaxy to worship Pharaoh Ramesses.' Amelia did not smile but just gazed at them with a blank look in her eyes.

'The Pharaoh will not be pleased. He ordered you to be fed to his favourite Nile crocodiles six months ago.'

That was news for Rex. Obviously, the future was not bright and rosy for him. He would have to resort to plan B – escape from hawk-headed robots and fix the past or maybe the future although he couldn't remember which right now since it was all a bit confusing. He looked at Panos, who was wondering if she had been (or was going to be) crocodile lunch too and winked at her. Panos decided it was time to implement Tremote tail use #375.

She whipped round her tail from behind her back holding her hand-blaster. A fraction of a second and three quick shots later and the three guard droids were twisted lumps of metal and melting plastic. Tremotes don't miss, especially with their tails. Amelia screamed loudly.

'Sorry Amelia, we are voluntarily excommunicating ourselves from the church of Rama.' Rex pushed her aside and ran for the exit. It was quiet outside with all the pilgrims still occupied inside. Two more burning hawk droids later and they were close to the landing pad. Rex used his communicator.

'Dennis, power up. Things getting messy. Get her airborne, we will be there in a minute.'

'Certainly, Sir Rex There are several security droids converging on our location. They are heavily armed. Can I deal with them ... please?' Dennis did not greatly appreciate other robots, particularly inferior models that had pretentious headgear. He had noticed that, as usual, Rama being a cheapskate had purchased outdated robots from the Syrus Droid

Foundries. They were probably surplus models on sale that he had adapted. Half-witted models that gave robots a bad name – good riddance. He rotated the ship's belly laser turret and blew away a handful of dumb hawk droids who were hanging around on the edge of the landing pad. For more fun he focused a full energy blast that fully disintegrated them and partially destroyed the right wing of the space terminal building. For some inexplicable reason deep within his circuits Dennis had always loved blowing things up.

'Well cool Dennis. Good shooting,' congratulated Jonny. Blowing up robots looked a great laugh. He desperately wanted a go but Dennis said no.

Rex and Panos stumbled, panting aboard and closed the hatch. A couple of seconds later and they were airborne.

Chapter Forty-Three

Federal Navy Midshipman Clarke aboard the renamed Sentinel Class Battlecruiser 'Hoth's Dream' was annoyed when the hot-line rang. He found the religious lunatics from the Thebian Planetary Defence Authority extremely irritating but not as much as the Captain did. The four of them had been playing cards.

'Pick it up Clarke. See what those crazy buggers want,' ordered Captain Murphy. He had a particularly bad hand of cards and would be pleased to see this round end soon. Planetary defence was the most boring posting he had ever had. There had been no enemies to fight since Ramesses had taken over. The tedium of day after day with nothing to do, except buzz a few boring pilgrim vessels and blow up a few errant asteroids, was getting to him.

'It's the Admiral Sir.' Clarke announced a bit surprised. What could he want? They had not heard from him for six months. The Admiral appeared menacingly in full dress uniform, his pompous, oversized epaulettes occupying most of the screen. A string of medals was crammed on to his chest from various space battles where, although he had not participated directly, he had send a large number of naval sailors to their death.

'Captain Murphy. This is a code red alert. A Vegan freighter has just left the atmosphere from Karnak. Please move to intercept.'

'Then what Sir?' asked Murphy. He hoped he would be allowed to blow the freighter away with the huge number of deadly weapons at his disposal. He crossed his fingers.

'Disable and capture. Caution the crew are dangerous. Then await further orders.' The Admiral's irritating holo-image disappeared.

Murphy decided he would blow them away anyway. Slowly not instantaneously that was more fun. Knock out the drives, puncture a few holes in the hull, watch a few crew members be sucked out into space and as a finale vaporise them with a full salvo of the Battlecruiser's energy weapons.

'Clarke tell the bridge to locate and intercept the vessel.' Clarke relayed the order to the bridge where the droid duty officer took over. With five 'organic' personnel and 75 droids the life-forms get a bit lazy. They went back to playing cards.

Chapter Forty-Four

The Eagle left the thick atmosphere of Thebes or 'The Pharonic Galactic Capital of the Wonderful Hoth' as it had been imaginatively rechristened and headed out of the planet's gravity well towards the hyperspace jump point.

'There is a Battlecruiser up our arse,' Rex noted. It was not totally unexpected but he had been hoping for a smaller naval pursuit vessel. 'How long to hyperspace Dennis?'

'At least 5.327 minutes Sir Rex.'

'And how long before the Battlecruiser is in range?'

'Less than one minute.'

'So, guys with the firepower on that thing we are at best vaporised into atoms or worst eating vacuum in about 1 minute 15 seconds,' Rex announced matter of factly. Rex knew that his shields, although good, were no match for one of the latest Sentinel Class Battlecruisers and his weaponry of laser cannons, meson accelerators and photonic torpedoes would probably not even penetrate the Battlecruiser's force shields. He considered engaging the Causal Flux Generator but without Dennis doing a detailed calculation he might finish up beneath the surface of Thebes or in one of its moons. Anyway, he had another plan.

In all things naval Rex had to admit he was a bit of a nerd. He kept onboard (hidden away from Panos who would just laugh at him) a small library about naval military history, great Federal star battles and best of all lots of warship statistics with those great numbered cutaway drawings. Unfortunately, modern interstellar conflict had become rather a tedious affair over the last 200 years. Gone were the days when daring, small ship raids counted or swashbuckling manoeuvres such as the Mangossian trick of teleporting a fusion bomb at close range into an enemy captain's stateroom toilet were used. Instead, rival navies had constructed large dreadnought armies of Battlecruisers with loads of long-range energy weapons and impenetrable force shields. They were crewed by droids to reduce casualties to 'real' people. Where was the fun and risk if hundreds of gasping Federation personnel could not be sucked into space on a hull breach? Giant fleets would line up facing each other and then slog it out at long range. The last one's shields to overload would be the winner. The looser would go 'pop' and disappear instantly in a scintillating cloud of interstellar gas.

Rex outgunned realised a swashbuckling manoeuvre would need to be reinvented. He quickly sat in the pilot's seat and switched the controls to manual. He pressed loads of buttons and switches that did nothing but made himself feel distinctly better. Jonny and the Professor were very impressed and felt for a split second that perhaps Rex had a sane plan and knew what he was up to.

'Bolt yourselves in guys. Here we go ...' He swung the ship around and hit the Vegan afterburners. There was slight jolt and everyone was pushed back as the ship's acceleration plates tried to compensate for the enormous thrust.

'What are you doing?' asked Jonny intrigued by seeing a real space battle at close hand.

Panos and Dennis did not need to ask. They already knew. Rex had discussed his theory, admittedly under the bravado effect of alcohol, many times. He had even had Dennis calculate the probabilities one day on a boring rainy afternoon.

'Since we are significantly outgunned, we are going to ram the enemy Battlecruiser. The Sentinel class has a very thin armour compared to the reinforced Nano-Combe Boride Titanium hull of the Eagle,' Dennis started to explain. He too was interested to check his calculations. Although with a statistical sample size of one he could not readily verify the probabilities he had painstakingly computed.

'Yea they are all tin-foil. Old solid technology will triumph over fancy quantum energy shields,' confirmed Rex. He was certain his plan would work. It had been forming in his mind for years.

Dennis continued his lecture. 'Based on optimal penetration speed the Battlecruiser will have less than ten seconds to fire on us before we collide with the upper control bridge. Our defence shields will last 12 seconds. We have a 25.7% chance of a clean penetration and a 52% chance of temporarily immobilising the Battlecruiser. In any case it will take them 10 minutes to transfer control to the secondary bridge.'

'Oh, I see.' Sounds dangerous thought Jonny. The Battlecruiser was no longer a small spec in space but was starting to hurtle closer towards them. Jonny could already make out the huge grey bulk bristling with gun turrets and deadly looking armaments. He guessed that the upper control bridge must be the superstructure poking conspicuously out from the Battlecruiser's triangular hull.

Chapter Forty-Five

'Captain it's the bridge. They say that the freighter has turned and is approaching to engage – although they have not energised weapons yet.'

'Really?' answered the Captain. He had a good hand. This was interrupting play.

'OK arm weapons. Prepare photonic torpedoes and short-range plasma cannons. Keep an eye on them.' He studied his cards closely. It was his turn. 'Put the phone down. Let's quickly finish the game and,' he paused, 'then have some fun obliterating the freighter.' He laughed.

The communicator rung again. They ignored it for a few seconds and then it abruptly stopped. The ship suddenly shook like it had been hit by a giant unseen hammer. A moment later an emergency alarm sounded down the nearby corridor. Safely bulkheads closed to prevent depressurisation. Panicking droids careered down the corridor.

The Eagle hit the Battlecruiser at high speed and passed though the bridge tower like an armour piercing bullet. Droids and equipment were sucked out into empty space. Rex felt pleased with himself – a swashbuckling manoeuvre that was worthy of the naval history books. But, unfortunately, nobody would read them because he was about to change history forever.

Chapter Forty-Six

Rex felt for a fleeting moment like an intergalactic rock star. He pulled his very dark stylish shades down and stepped into the press room. There was a blaze of flashing cameras from a hundred of the Galaxy's best-known sports journalists. Two men left in the final of the Extreme X Cup and he was one of them. He was somehow a hairs breadth away from winning five billion Andurian crypto-dollars, the hardest currency in the known Universe. He would be minted forever and it probably would be forever if he used Rama's regenerative consultant and avoided any more extreme sports tournaments.

Anyway, he unfortunately now had more important concerns than actually winning the final. He had the known Galaxy to save. He reluctantly pushed visions of sporty aircars, luxurious villas and sleek star-yachts from his mind.

Elmer Diablilo entered from the other side of the press room and sat calmly at the other end of the table. Totally emotionless, cool as a cucumber thought Rex.

'Captain Rogers, how do you feel about the Thor Paragliding Event? How do you rate your chances?' asked a reporter.

'Feeling good. Hopefully I won't lose a foot on this one,' he laughed. He tried to inject some humour into the proceedings.

'A question from the Galactic Sports Daily. Some or our readers feel you have qualified by just being lucky. You almost flew into a cliff on the jet-pack event.'

'Yea lucky I guess,' he thought of his current predicament, '... sometimes.'

'Elmer you have scored the highest points consistently throughout this tournament. You are the favourite. What are thinking?' asked another reporter.

'I am the best and I am going to win,' Elmer announced. No doubt in his voice.

There was something very wrong with Diablilo, Rex thought. He could not put his finger on it. Was he on medication?

The interviews continued for a few minutes in a similar inane vein. Rex looked out of the hotel pressroom windows at the Thor larva fields stretching out beneath them. One last crazy event – paragliding over highly active volcano vents. The five billion dollars prize money popped briefly back into his mind again but he had to forget about his personal spending plans and fix the future for everyone else. In one hour, Rama and his friendly statue would try and take over most of the known Galaxy. Trillions of harmless Federal citizens would be reduced to days of slavery, poverty and endless worship of a demented pan-dimensional deity. Only he seemingly could change the course of history. Panos and the others should be back at Thebes by now. He had instructed them what to do.

Chapter Forty-Seven

The paragliding event across the Vents of Thor was a head-to-head event. Both he and Diablilo would lift off at the same time for the 30 mile glide across the broken larva surface of the volcano cone. The first to the finish would win. Although the fabric of the hang gliders was somewhat heat resistant a larva flare from one of the vents would prove fatal.

Rama was at the start and presided over what was left of the newly purged Extreme X Cup Organising Committee. Apparently Blofield Blatus had been unable to attend due to a serious stomach infection. Speculation had arisen in the media that the hotel food on Thebes was to blame. Always a man for the theatrical Rama was dressed in his full Pharaoh's regalia and holding the ancient sceptre. He smiled weakly at Rex as Rex checked his harness. Rama's eyes were a bit glassy and he looked pale and not like himself.

The starting droid quickly commenced the countdown. 'Ready gentlemen? 3, 2, 1 ... set, go!'

Elmer Diablilo jumped off the rocky rim of the volcano. Instead, to every one's surprise, including Rama's, Rex unclipped his harness and ran towards Rama and grabbed the sceptre.

'Sorry Rama but you aren't qualified to run the Galaxy. Stick to hotels.' He pushed Rama to the ground.

'Stop him ...' protested Rama, desperately trying to hold onto the sceptre. He flailed around helplessly, hampered by his cumbersome Egyptian robes. Rex tore the sceptre from him, ran back to the hang glider and jumped. Within seconds Rex was far away from the crater's edge and heading towards the larva fields below. He needed to find a suitably big larva vent to dispose of the sceptre.

Chapter Forty-Eight

On Thebes Jonny took Dennis to the temple he had seen being constructed near the waterpark. They passed tourists in swimming costumes carrying towels on their way back to the hotel. A few construction droids were diligently completing the pathway and a hawk-headed guard robot stood outside.

'Wait here Jonny. It will be safer.'

'What's the plan?' asked Jonny eagerly.

'Well, it's kind of totally beneath me but I will impersonate a security droid and steal the Statue of Hoth,' explained Dennis. 'Very easy I'm afraid. It's the optimum plan I have computed.'

'That's it?' Jonny thought it was a great plan but a bit disappointed by the simplicity of it. He really wanted a dangerous break-in with a shoot-out or something equally dramatic.

'Don't worry,' reassured Dennis, 'we will have some fun after.'

As Jonny watched Dennis transmuted before eyes from Robby the Robot to a frightening hawk-headed security guard. He then walked towards the temple. The security guard ignored him as he passed by and he entered the temple. Inside there was a couple of loud bangs and flashes. Dennis appeared a few minutes later with a casket under one arm and a large laser cannon in the other. The security guard levelled his weapon but not before Dennis had blown its head clean off its shoulders.

'I have it. Let's go,' said Dennis. Before leaving he decided that a bit more wanton destruction could be allowed under the circumstances.

'Watch this,' he said as he meticulously blew up five of the six columns supporting the portico. He left the central sixth pillar for Jonny to destroy who decided, as the front of the temple collapsed, that blowing things up for real was much more fun than computer games.

They hurried back to the ship. The Professor and Panos were anxiously waiting in the engine room. The cask containing the statue fitted neatly in the empty hamster cage on the bench. Jonny thought he heard a muffled howl of protestation from inside the cask but perhaps he was imagining.

'Here we go. Au revoir Mr. Hoth,' said Professor Mitchell. They stood back and engaged the Causal Flux Generator. The contents of the casket flickered, shimmered and disappeared.

'The hamsters can have their cage back now Jonny,' said Panos smiling.

Chapter Forty-Nine

Rex flew dangerously over a large larva vent. In the giant crevasse he could see the molten lava bubbling away. The volcanic gases blew against his hang-glider buffeting it in a scorching hot wind. He hoped there would be no eruption from the vent in the next few minutes. Although his pressure suit protected him from the noxious gases, he could already feel the blistering heat. He threw the sceptre down into the vent and watched as it spiralled downwards to be engulfed in the larva below. He then turned and set off carefully towards the finish on the other side of the crater.

Elmer Diablilo was a long way ahead and landed well before Rex. He walked over and congratulated Rex in a strange Elmer Diablilo way.

'Well done. Too bad you came second. The better man won though,' he smiled and walked off. Something not quite right with that guy Rex thought to himself again.

The media crowded round him. More cameras and interviews. He had missed the big prize money but he could probably make some money from interviews and selling some of that Egyptian junk he had brought back from the tomb. But at least he had foiled Rama's little plan. He looked round for Rama. It appeared he had had a big televised tantrum and had immediately left the planet in a huff. Rex still wanted to have words with him about the poker game stitch-up.

Chapter Fifty

The tall man with the 'Extreme X Cup' T-shirt and the tweedy looking Professor type sat at the end of the bar. To the annoyance of the other customers, they had propped their wet surfboard against the counter.

'What do you guys want to drink?' asked Jonny from behind the bar.

'I think we both deserve a nice cold beer, don't you?' answered Rex. He was feeling more relaxed now he was back in St. Ives. All his problems with mad Pharaohs, hungry Pterodactyls and meddlesome minor deities disguised as statues seemed far away.

Jonny's dad entered from the kitchen. 'Where have you been? Skiving off for the afternoon?' he smiled.

Jonny didn't know what to say, 'Umm ... well just helping these guys out.'

'Good. Well serve them a beer ... oh and no surfboards on the bar.' He was in a hurry and went out to the terrace.

'Well have you given it to him yet?' quizzed the surfboard. It was the best amphibious disguise Dennis could think of at short notice. The lack of legs or wheels was bothersome though. A crocodile had come to mind but he thought that was perhaps inappropriate for a crowded Cornish beach.

'No, just about to.' Rex reached into his pocket and handed Jonny a small, gilded box.

'What's this?' said Jonny. He picked it up and carefully opened it. Inside was a thick gold medal with a hologram of a surfer and a large wave emblazoned on it. The closer he looked the more the surfer looked like him.

'The Extreme X Cup Surf Award,' said Rex. 'You won the second round remember?'

'And was almost eaten by a shark?' laughed the surfboard, vibrating slightly and sloshing the beer around.

'Wow that really is cool. A surf medal!' Jonny was awed. A medal. An interstellar surf medal. Unique in the whole world, even the whole Galaxy!

'Well, you did rather well too Rex?' enthused the Professor. He had become addicted to following the holo-vision coverage of the Extreme X Cup. He had discovered a whole new universe of trashy sports and reality shows to fill his evenings with.

'Second place!' whined Rex. 'I get a poxy medal. No offense Jonny. A few advertising and product endorsement offers,' but this was the annoying bit, 'I missed the prize money.'

'Diablilo was very good. Probably unbeatable,' said the Professor. 'The perfect competitor.' He always enthusiastically listened to the commentary and frequently regurgitated the pundits' opinions.

'Yes, they wanted me to do it,' said matter of factly Dennis.

Rex stunned looked at Dennis. 'What do you mean exactly?' queried Rex.

'Well, he is a robot like me. In fact, the same model as me. They only made two of us,' answered Dennis. He could not see what the fuss was about. 'The real Elmer Diablilo retired last year. He is I believe on a interstellar cruise liner somewhere.'

'How come?' spluttered Rex. He knew there was something wrong with Diablilo. No droids, life-forms only in the Extreme X Cup. That was the rules. They even had a medical at the start of the tournament.

'Yes, well you won me off Lazard Bond, remember? And he was very annoyed by all accounts. He had to order a new DENNIS droid at the last minute.'

'Yea that was before they all started cheating ...' Rex was still annoyed with those poker scumbags. Now he was positively mad. He involuntarily started to grind his teeth.

'Yes, I understand that Diablilo was due to be paid a cut of the prize money.'

'And you somehow didn't think it was worth telling me he was a droid?' Rex was visibly annoyed with Dennis. Morally only he was allowed to cheat and get away with it.

'You didn't ask Sir Rex. I just thought it was obvious.'

Rex glugged down the rest of his beer and made for the door, surfboard under his arm. He deliberately bumped the surfboard against the door frame.

'See you soon Jonny ... there are urgent things to sort out.'

Chapter Fifty-One

Paranessu had been searching for a couple of hours for the stupid goat amidst the reeds of the Nile delta. His dad would be annoyed with him again for his incompetence. He only had a few goats to look after and had fallen asleep on the job. It was very hot but his dad Seti was an important soldier and thought that everybody should be as efficient as him. Paranessu knew he was worth more than looking after a few silly goats. One day he would be a famous general or maybe even a great Pharaoh. He had dreamt this more than once recently. He saw the goat; it was chewing happily on some lush bush. Walking towards it he noticed a shattered metal casket lying in the mud. Beside it was a black, obsidian statue. It had a jackal head, a bit like the god Anubis thought Paranessu. He picked it up and looked at it – its eyes were like black pits, stars shone beguilingly in them. A mesmerising voice entered his head.

'Paranessu. You will be great and powerful ... I will help you. You will be the Pharaoh Ramesses. Ramesses I.'

A smile spread over Paranessu's face. It sounded better than chasing goats every day.

Hoth felt the child had ambition and desire for power. He was a good candidate. Although deep down the conversation felt somewhat familiar. He could not remember. Had he been here before?

THE END

Table of Contents

Chapter One..7

Chapter Two..9

Chapter Three..11

Chapter Four..17

Chapter Five...21

Chapter Six...23

Chapter Seven...25

Chapter Eight...27

Chapter Nine..31

Chapter Ten...33

Chapter Eleven..35

Chapter Twelve...37

Chapter Thirteen...39

Chapter Fourteen..41

Chapter Fifteen...43

Chapter Sixteen..47

Chapter Seventeen...51

Chapter Eighteen..55

Chapter Nineteen...57

Chapter Twenty……………………………...………59

Chapter Twenty-one………………………...……….63

Chapter Twenty-two………………………….....…..65

Chapter Twenty-three……………………….....…...67

Chapter Twenty-four……………………………..…69

Chapter Twenty-Five…………………………….….71

Chapter Twenty-Six……………………………...…73

Chapter Twenty-Seven……………………………..75

Chapter Twenty-Eight……………………………...77

Chapter Twenty-Nine……………………………....79

Chapter Thirty……………………………………...81

Chapter Thirty-One………………………………...85

Chapter Thirty-Two………………………………..87

Chapter Thirty-Three……………………………...89

Chapter Thirty-Four……………………………....97

Chapter Thirty-Five………………………………109

Chapter Thirty-Six………………………………...111

Chapter Thirty-Seven……………………………...113

Chapter Thirty-Eight………………………………115

Chapter Thirty-Nine……………………………....119

Chapter Forty……………………………………123

Chapter Forty-One..127
Chapter Forty-Two..131
Chapter Forty-Three..137
Chapter Forty-Four...139
Chapter Forty-Five...143
Chapter Forty-Six..145
Chapter Forty-Seven..147
Chapter Forty-Eight..149
Chapter Forty-Nine...151
Chapter Fifty..153
Chapter Fifty-One..157

Printed by Printforce, United Kingdom